# blurred lines

an *Out of Line* novel

# blurred
# lines

an *Out of Line* novel

**Jen McLaughlin**

Manufactured in the United States of America

Print ISBN: 978-0-9907819-0-5

Edited by: Kristin at Coat of Polish Edits
Copy edited by: Hollie Westring
Cover Designed by: Sarah Hansen at © OkayCreations.net
Interior Design and Formatting by: Tianne Samson with E.M. Tippetts Book Designs

# Books by
# Jen McLaughlin

**Out of Line Series:**
*Out of Line*
*Out of Time*
*Out of Mind*
*Out of Line Box Set* (Out of Line 1-3)
*Fractured Lines*
*Blurred Lines*

*Between Us*


Written as Diane Alberts:

**Take a Chance Series:**
*Try Me (Take a Chance #1)*
*Love Me (Take a Chance #2)*
*Play Me (Take a Chance #3)*
*Take Me (Take a Chance #4)*

*Seducing the Princess*
*Stealing His Heart*
*Falling for the Groomsman*
*Faking It*
*Divinely Ruined*
*On One Condition*
*Broken*
*Kiss Me At Midnight*
*Kill Me Tomorrow*
*Temporarily Yours*
*Reclaimed*


**Superstars in Love Series:**
*Captivated by You*
*One Night*

*For Jay. I love you, girl.*

*Once burned...*

Finding my fiancée naked on my couch might've been a good thing, if her ex-boyfriend hadn't been with her. For the past eight years I've been a witness to the power of true love, but after getting burned I'd decided there wasn't any hope for me finding it for myself. Until I met Noelle Brandt in a hotel bar. Maybe it wasn't the most romantic meeting, but the moment I met her I knew I had to have her. The more I learn about her, the more I know I'll do whatever it takes to keep her.

*Twice shy...*

I'd already found the love of my life, but I'd lost that love forever. And I'd been lost ever since. But one night a wounded man makes all of that go away. He makes me laugh, live, and feel alive. When he tells me he has no intention of letting me go, I finally begin to believe in the power of true love again. That is, until I find out who he really is...and by then, it's far too late to correct the mistakes we've already made.

By the time we both know the truth, the lines have already been blurred beyond recognition.

## *An Excerpt from Blurred Lines…*

Her eyes drifted shut. Warning bells went off in my head. I wasn't supposed to start anything with her, damn it. She'd been kind, and she deserved kindness in return.

That's all I had been trying to do. Be kind.

But then she closed her eyes, and lifted up on her toes…and all my good intentions flew out the window. Lowering my head slowly, giving her plenty of time to push me away or turn her head aside, I moved closer until my lips were almost touching hers. "Tell me to stop if you don't want this."

"Riley…" She inhaled a shaky breath, her fists tightening on my shirt. "Don't feel like you have to do this as a thank you."

"I shouldn't be doing this, because you deserve better." I tightened my grip on her and caught her behind her waist, hauling her closer. Her large breasts pushed against my chest, and I groaned. "Never mistake this for what it is: the greedy actions of a greedy man. I want you. I know I shouldn't take you, but yet…"

"You want to?" she asked, her wet lips begging to be kissed. "I want to, too."

I dropped my forehead to hers. "Why?"

"I don't know," she admitted. She undid another button. "But I do."

"Noelle…"

"I didn't bring you up here for this," she said breathlessly. "I don't mind that it's happening, but I didn't bring you up here to seduce you."

"And I didn't come here to seduce *you*." I brushed my lips across hers, barely touching. "Which is why I should stop."

"Or not."

She tipped her face up, and I kissed her fully, without overthinking it. The second our lips touched, the world as I knew it changed all around me. Yeah, it sounded corny as shit coming from a guy, but it was true.

So fucking *true*.

# chapter
# one

### Riley

I parked my car in the driveway and just sat there, staring up at the house I shared with my fiancée, Sarah. It was dark outside, and somewhere in the distance, a dog barked. It sounded pissed as hell, but that wasn't why I didn't get out of the car. It wasn't why I was sitting here, feeling empty as hell and just as lost.

The truth was, I wasn't going inside because I knew my fiancée wasn't in there alone. I'd seen the car parked down the road, conveniently hidden behind large shrubbery. If I was any other man, it might have worked. I might not have noticed it when I drove by on my way to my next meeting. But I'd know that fucking car anywhere.

It was Sarah's ex-boss's car.

The same one she'd once dated.

When we'd met, they'd been freshly split up. He'd broken her heart, and she'd sworn him off forever. We'd dated a suitable amount of time before getting engaged. My parents had liked her, and so had I. It had been an arranged marriage of sorts, but in my circles, that wasn't such a strange thing.

Our fathers were political affiliates. We were expected to marry. Once upon a time, I'd hoped to have more. I'd hoped to have the kind of love that consumed your soul.

I still hadn't found it.

So, I'd asked Sarah to marry me. She'd said yes. I'd thought she loved me. I'd been fairly certain I would grow to love her. But if she really loved me...

Why the hell was her ex-boyfriend's car outside my house?

Slowly, I opened my car door and made my way up the driveway. My heart thudded in my ears, and I knew what I'd find when I opened that door. There was no doubt my fiancée was naked and having sex with another man.

And yet, I went inside anyway.

The door creaked when it opened, and I froze, half expecting to hear frantic shouting and retreating footsteps. Nothing moved. I crept inside the rest of the way, leaving the front door open. As I walked, I found a man's sweater on the floor. I stepped on it. Another step and I scored a pair of men's pants and a skirt.

There was no doubt anymore, if there ever had been, that my fiancée was cheating on me. I didn't need to go any farther. I had confirmation. But still...

I kept going.

For some reason, I needed to see it with my own eyes to believe it. I'd truly believed Sarah was an honest woman. One who wouldn't sleep with someone behind my back. I'd thought she would be a good partner for life. A trustworthy one.

I reached the couch. The couch *I'd* picked out.

Sarah was kneeling between her ex's feet. She was naked, and so was her ex. The man's bare ass was on *my* fucking couch. I didn't know what upset me more: that, or the fact that she was giving the dude a BJ.

She never did that with me. Said it was undignified.

So was fucking a dude on my couch.

And, yes, I knew that the fact that those two things bothered me just as much as the actual betrayal did was fucked up. But I hadn't loved her. I'd wanted to...

But I didn't really know what real love felt like.

Fisting my hands, I cleared my throat. "I'm home early."

Sarah shrieked and flew to her feet, grabbing the throw blanket off the arm of my couch and covering her body with it. Which was absurd, really. We'd both seen her naked before, *obviously*. The man also stood, grabbing a pillow and covering his half-hard dick with it.

"You can keep that now," I said drily, not taking my eyes off Sarah. She was pale and shaking. I forced myself to remain calm. To act as if this hadn't completely taken me off guard, even if it hadn't broken me like it should have. "So, I take it the engagement is off, then?"

"Riley, I'm so sorry." Tears streamed down her cheeks. "I didn't want you to see this..."

"Obviously," I said. "Cheaters rarely do."

She shook her head, her blonde hair flying everywhere. "No. I'm not a cheater. I just—"

"Seriously?" I threw my arms out. "If this isn't cheating, what the hell do you call it?"

Her cheeks flushed. "I love him, Riley. *Really* love him."

I froze then, absorbing the knowledge that she'd felt the same way about me that I felt about her—and I hadn't even known it. I'd naïvely thought she actually loved me, instead of just, well, accepting me as a suitable partner. How had I missed that?

"I thought you loved me," I said softly, scratching my head. "I didn't know..."

"I do." She came up to me, resting her hand on my heart. The same hand that had been cupping another man's balls moments before. That skeeved me out, so I stepped back from her touch. "I love you, Riley."

"But you're not in love with me," I said, swallowing hard.

I might not love her till my dying breath, but the reality of what was happening hit me pretty hard. We were together for three fucking years, and it was over now. We'd just mailed the wedding invitations out last week.

And she'd been fucking him.

"I'm sorry," she whispered, tears falling down her cheeks.

I had no doubt she was. She was always a nice person, which was why this came as such a shock. I never suspected this of her. Hell, we'd made love last night, and she'd spent half an hour talking about wedding dresses and centerpieces.

I locked eyes with her bright green ones. "When did this start?"

"Riley..."

"*When?*"

She crumbled. "A week ago."

The dude finally spoke up. He took a step forward. "Look, man, I'm sorry, but—"

Without thinking, I cocked my fist back and punched him right in the fucking face. He'd broken her heart, and now he was going to do it again. She might think he'd changed, but any man who would fuck another man's fiancée on his own couch was not a changed man. He was scum, pure and simple.

And she'd fallen for him again.

"Don't speak to me," I snarled. I went after him, even though he stumbled backward and tripped over a fallen pillow. "Don't you ever fucking—"

"Riley, don't!" Sarah called out, sobbing. "Please. Don't hurt him."

I fisted my hands, my breathing coming out harsh. She'd cheated on me with this lowlife, and she was worried *I'd* hurt *him*? I whirled on her. "If you loved me, even if you weren't *in* love with me, you wouldn't have done this, Sarah. Not to me."

She covered her face and cried. "I'm sorry."

"Yeah." I shook my head. "You made a big mistake, Sarah. I would have treated you right. I never would have...never...I wouldn't have done this."

"But you don't love me," she whispered. "You never have."

"I care about you. I respect you." I looked at her again. "I would have treated you right. That's more important than love. And it's safer, too."

"I know," she said, shrugging hopelessly. "I wanted more, though."

And she thought she'd find it with this guy? I looked at him again. He sat on the floor, butt-assed naked and shaking. Pathetic. Turning my attention back to her, I forced a calm smile. My lawyer smile, as I liked to call it.

The one that said: *I have no problem with taking your ass to court and whooping it publicly, so you better enter a plea bargain.* I'd never given it to her before.

"Well, then, I wish you the best of luck. Goodbye."

Sarah stumbled after me, grabbing my arm. "Wait. What will we tell everyone?"

"Tell them whatever you want." I shook off her hold. "I don't care."

She grabbed for me again, but I pulled back. "But—"

"I said I don't care, okay?" I held my hands up. "You were right about one thing—I never loved you. So, I don't give a damn what you say to them."

She covered her mouth and cried. I felt nothing. Not really.

But I didn't want her touching me. Not anymore. This was the second time I'd found my significant other in bed with another man. The first time had been in college, and it had hurt like hell. I'd actually loved her...or I'd thought I had, anyway.

Now I was starting to think I was incapable of love.

Sure, I'd loved a girl once, but she hadn't loved me back. She'd been in love with her now-husband, and they were the only couple I knew actually in love. Like, the kind you see in movies. Finn and Carrie had it, but I never would. Not in this lifetime.

I stumbled out the door, tugging on my tie as I went. It felt tight. As if it had come to life and decided to choke what little life I had left out of me. I was tempted to let it.

I was stuck in a job I hated, at a firm my father owned, and now I was single, too. And for the second time in my life, I'd been duplicitously cheated on.

Was it something I'd done? Something that was missing in me that made my women look elsewhere? Maybe I was broken. Maybe I should stop trying to find a partner and just accept the fact that I was better off alone.

Maybe I should just stop trying.

But first? I'd call off the meeting that I was already late to...and I'd get drunk as hell as quickly as possible. I'd get so drunk that I'd forget all about Sarah and the naked man on my couch. So drunk that I'd forget all about how broken I was, because instead of being heartbroken over her betrayal, I was angry that we'd have to deal with the mess she'd made.

I was mad I'd have to tell my mother that I was no longer marrying the woman she'd handpicked for me, and deal with the drama that came with it all. But I wasn't upset I lost *her*...

Not at all.

# chapter two

## Noelle

"Come on, just one more drink?" said my best friend and fellow author. "Then I'll let you go upstairs to get some work done."

We sat in the lavish hotel lobby, which doubled as a bar. The hotel bar was packed, and the voices bounced off the walls in some sort of competition with the aerodynamics of the room. There wasn't an empty seat in the house, and some people were even camped out on the floor. I was in San Diego for a writer's conference, and I was having a blast. I really was.

But the bar was packed to the gills, and it was a competition to be heard in the crowd. It was almost as if everyone was competing with one another as to who could shout the loudest. And I was losing horribly. It was an introvert's nightmare...and I was one of the worst of them. But, hey, at least I admitted it.

That had to count for something.

All I wanted to do was kick off these heels, put on a pair of comfy pajamas, and lose myself in an episode of *Sons of Anarchy*. I was in need of some Jax therapy.

"I don't want to work," I shouted into her ear. That much was true at least. "I'm just tired and want to lay down in my hotel room with no noise."

Except Jax. And I'd fibbed a bit. I wasn't tired at all. Thanks to three macchiatos in the hotel Starbucks earlier, I was like a hamster in a wheel, spinning round and round and round. I just wanted to do it within the safety of my cage...

In this case, my hotel room. I scanned the crowded room, seeing so many familiar faces. But there was one that didn't fit. I sipped my wine and nudged Emily's ribs. "Hey. One of these things is not like the other. Which is it?"

She sipped her wine and then almost choked on it. "Holy shit."

I nodded, not needing to speak to show my agreement. We were beyond that point. We were telepathically connected, so she knew exactly what I was thinking. All the time. And if we weren't magically connected somehow, then we were just weird. Which was perfectly fine with me.

Weird was cool.

I focused on the anomaly again. He seemed oblivious to the attention, but that wasn't exactly a shocker. On a scale of one to ten, he was a twenty. He wore an expensive-looking suit and sat at the bar alone, seemingly completely unaware he was in the midst of a room full of romance writers, editors, and bloggers.

His broad shoulders were unbelievably strong, his slightly messy blond hair begged to be touched, and he had muscles like whoa. His brown leather briefcase sat at his feet, and he drank what looked like whiskey. He downed it like there was no tomorrow, and he immediately lifted his hand for another.

He didn't even glance my way.

For some reason, I couldn't look away.

"Who do you think he is? A cover model?" Emily whispered, lifting her glass of wine to her lips again. "An author? An editor? A porn star?"

I rolled my eyes at the last one. "Or just a random dude," I said, downing the last of my wine. "There are people in this hotel who aren't in the romance industry, I'm sure."

"Yeah, maybe..." Emily pursed her lips. "But he looks like a cover model."

He did. He was totally hotter than the ones I'd seen here so far, that was for sure. There was a reason the majority of romance book covers were headless, thank you very much. But this guy was hot in that effortless way that made women quiver and rip their clothes off within seconds of meeting him. In other words?

He was way outta my league.

I probably wouldn't even be able to get a freaking word out in his presence. Good thing I had no intention of trying. "He's definitely gorgeous, but we'll never find out who he is." I stood up. "Okay, time for me to—"

Someone tapped my shoulder. "Excuse me? Aren't you K.M. Reed?"

Forcing a smile, I turned around and talked to the woman behind me. She was one of my favorite authors, and on any other day I'd be hopping up and down on one foot because I was actually talking to her. But right now, I was fresh outta enthusiasm.

And the last drink I'd drunk had hit me *hard*.

By the time we finished chatting and I said my goodbyes, the world was spinning. I headed for the elevator, rummaging in my purse for my keycard as I went. After pushing the button for my floor, I glanced up when someone cleared their throat, the usual friendly smile on my face.

But when I saw who it was I froze. It was *him*. The hot guy from the bar. And he was looking at me, the intensity of his bright green eyes locked solely on me.

*Cracker jacks.*

"Hi," he said.

"Uh…" I said.

He looked at me a little closer, squinting in that way drunk people did when they were trying to stop seeing two of something. It never worked. "What did you say?"

What had I said? Shit. I didn't know. I swallowed hard. "I said hi. I think."

"Oh." He leaned against the wall…and almost toppled over. He barely caught himself. "You don't happen to be checking out, are you?"

That didn't make any sense, grammatically speaking, so it took me a second to answer. "Uh…no. Why?"

"Because I'm drunk as hell," he slurred. He switched his briefcase to his left hand. He had strong fingers. I could tell by the way he gripped the handles. Also, no wedding ring. Not that I was looking or anything. "And I have nowhere to go. I thought there would be a room available, so I drank. A lot. Like, a hell of a lot. Enough to put an alcoholic under the table. But there's some convention here, and I can't get a room now."

He was so drunk that he said *convention* as *contention*. It was adorable, and it made him a heck of a lot more approachable than I'd ever thought possible. "It's a romance writer's conference. Didn't you notice all the women in the bar staring at you?"

"No." He blinked. "I didn't see anyone at all."

Okay then. "Are you from out of town?"

"No. I live here. Or, I lived here, I guess. Now I don't know where

I live anymore." He stared off into the distance. He looked so lost and sad and *ugh*. So freaking irresistible. "I have nowhere to go. I hadn't thought of that when I left."

My heart pinged a little bit at his sad, lost puppy-dog eyes. I didn't even think he was trying to look so darn adorable, but he was. He really was. And he had nowhere to go. That brought out all kinds of sympathy in my half-drunk heart. There was something about this guy, something I couldn't put my finger on, that called for me to listen. To care. Which was kind of crazy, really.

Maybe I needed to cut back on the wine.

"What happened to your house?" I asked, cocking my head. "Why can't you go back to it?"

"Well, it had another naked man in it." He looked at me again, the clarity in his eyes that hadn't been there before hitting me hard. "And my fiancée naked, too."

My heart wrenched. Well, that explained why he was here drinking alone and not looking at any other women. He was too busy grieving to realize he'd been surrounded by hundreds of women. Poor guy. "I'm sorry."

"Yeah. Me too. We made sense, her and I. We just did. And it was safe, you know. Sensible and safe." The elevator doors opened, and he looked at it as if it was about to attack. He stood in front of me — protecting me, maybe? — blinking at it. "Holy shit. Did you push the button?"

"Yeah." My lips twitched. I had no idea what he was like sober, but drunk — he was cute as hell. "What are you going to do now?"

He held the doors open for me when they started to shut. "I have no idea, but you better go up to your room, Ms. ...?" He squinted at my badge. He shouldn't have bothered, because it had my pen name on it, not my real one. "Uh..."

"Brandt. Noelle Brandt."

He squinted a bit more, as if he couldn't figure out why the name didn't match my badge, and shook his head. "Nice to meet you, Ms. Brandt." He bowed to me and almost fell over before straightening and pressing a hand to his chest. "Shit. I better not do that again. Forgive my matters."

I choked on a laugh. "You mean manners?"

"Yeah. Those." He tugged on his unbuttoned collar, his green eyes locked on me. His hair was standing up on end even more now. "Thanks for the conversation. I think I needed that."

"You're welcome. Bye. Uh, good luck."

"Thanks," he said, offering me a small smile. He still had his arm up, holding the doors for me, and I could see how hard and solid he was. Emily was right. He could totally be a cover model. "Good night."

I walked past him, every nerve in me wanting to stay. There was just something about him. I didn't know him, but I had a feeling that he had a habit of always helping people...and now he needed someone to help *him*.

I stopped halfway in the elevator. Directly in front of him, my heart sped up at the close proximity. Up close, he was even cuter. How was that possible? I didn't think it was. "Where will you go?"

"I don't know," he answered honestly.

His eyes looked even greener up close and personal, and he smelled like sinful sex. That might not make sense, but he did. His gaze moved over my face slowly, as if he was seeing me for the first time. He forced his attention back to my eyes, but by then my heart was already racing ridiculously fast.

"Hey," I whispered.

"Hey." Reaching out, he tugged on a strand of my hair. "You have blue in your hair. I like it."

I'd dyed it on a whim before coming here. Just one strand, but he'd noticed. "Come up to my room with me," I blurted out before I fully realized I'd been planning on saying it. "I mean, I have an extra bed. My roommate dropped out last minute."

Wait. Had I actually just invited a strange man up to my room?

His jaw flexed. "I couldn't."

"Why not?"

"I wouldn't want anyone to get the wrong idea," he said, motioning toward the bar full of women. "Don't you have friends out there?"

"Yes." I looked over my shoulder. No one was watching us. "It doesn't matter, though. No one would care. Why would they? I'm a big girl."

He grabbed my hand and ran his thumb over my ring finger. "Won't your husband mind?"

"My—?" I looked down at my ring. The ring I'd never taken off. How had he noticed that in his state? "Oh. I'm not...he's..."

I didn't finish.

"He's what?" He blinked at me, then a look of comprehension hit him. He reached out and squeezed my shoulder. "Divorce or...?"

"He's dead," I said flatly, the pain now a dull shaft instead of a sharp knife. "Has been for more than a year and a half. I just haven't taken it off. Sentimentality and all."

"I'm so sorry," he rasped. "I didn't mean to..."

"It's fine, really." I shook off the familiar loneliness that came when I talked about Roger. "But we can be sorry together. I have an empty bed. You can have it."

"You don't even know my name." He stumbled a little bit. "For all you know, I could be a serial killer, and you're inviting me in."

"If you were a serial killer, you wouldn't have reminded me of that." I stepped behind him and shoved him into the elevator because he was coming up with me. End of story. He fell into the open space, hitting the wall with a loud groan. "Oops. Sorry about that."

"*You* might be the serial killer," he mumbled, rubbing his abused shoulder.

"Maybe." The doors closed behind us. "I've been called a killer of hopes and dreams once or twice when I didn't end my books the way readers wanted."

He blinked. "You write books?"

"Yep. Romance books." I tucked my hair behind my ear. "And I'm a blogger, too."

He leaned on the elevator wall, his forehead adorably wrinkled. Even drunk off his ass and drunkenly stupid the man was hot. And he didn't seem to know it. It wasn't fair. Something about him looked familiar, but I couldn't place him. "A *what*?"

"A—" I cut myself off. "Never mind."

"You write romance books?" he asked, grinning sloppily. "Mother would just *love* that."

I lifted my chin. That sounded a little too judgmental to me. "I do."

"That's awesome. Seriously."

I relaxed a bit. "Thanks. I like it."

"Good." The doors opened, and he blinked at them again. It seemed as if he'd just remembered where we were going and why. "I don't know if I should do this. It feels wrong."

"Why? Are you going to kill me in my sleep?"

"No. Of course not." He ran his fingers through his hair. Is that why it was standing on end? "But I don't even know you. And you don't know me."

"We know enough."

He stood in front of the doors, keeping them open. I was half worried he'd fall asleep like that. He looked exhausted. "What's my name?"

"Why don't you tell me? I told you mine."

He dropped his arm to his side and closed his eyes, yawning. "Riley."

"Hello, Riley." I held my hand out. "Nice to meet you."

He opened his eyes, stared at me, and slid his hand into mine. As soon as we touched, I swear electric sparks shot out of our hands. He seemed to notice it, too, because he straightened and stared at our joined hands with wide eyes. Then he looked back up at me, and the heat in his eyes took my breath away. Legit *took my breath away*.

"Nice to meet you, too." His lips tipped into a smile. Had I thought it was hard to breathe before? Hell no. It was hard to breathe now. The man was a weapon of mass destruction, and he didn't even know it. "But I'm still not going into your room with you."

"Why not?"

He cocked a brow. "I already said why not."

I held my hand out again, locking eyes with him. "Look, believe it or not, I don't make it a habit to invite men I just met into my hotel room. Like, ever."

"I didn't say you did," he said quickly, running a hand down his face. "Not that there's anything wrong with that if you did. I mean, this is America."

I choked on a laugh. "Yeah, but I don't. And I won't." I took a deep breath, wiggling my fingers at him. "But I'm a good judge of character, and my gut is saying you need a friend tonight. Let me be that friend. I swear I won't ravish you in your sleep, kill you, or mug you. Don't let the blue streak fool you. I'm actually pretty lame."

He stared at me for so long that I thought he might refuse. But after a few silent moments, he took a step forward and slid his fingers into mine. "You don't look lame to me."

I didn't know what to say to that, but for the second time that night, he took my breath away. He probably didn't even know it. "Thanks."

"No, thank you, Ms. Brandt." Raising my hand to his lips, he kissed it ever so lightly. "You're like an angel sent to save me tonight, aren't you?"

Ignoring my body's enthusiastic response to his mouth on my skin, I rolled my eyes and led him toward my room. "If you knew me, you'd know how ludicrous that statement is."

"You might not be an angel, but you're mine."

That made no sense, but I understood what he meant. I didn't know what to say, so I said nothing at all. He leaned on the wall as I unlocked my door. After it beeped, he opened it for me, smiling at me as I went inside. And I knew…I just knew…

That I'd started something real tonight.

Something not even *I* fully comprehended.

# chapter three

## Riley

I walked into the room, my mind racing as fast as it could with almost a bottle's worth of whiskey floating around and mixing things up. I didn't know much right now, but I knew one thing. No matter what happened, I couldn't touch this woman. This romance writer, Noelle Brandt. She'd shown me nothing but kindness when I'd needed it most.

And showing her anything besides respect would be wrong.

There was something about her that demanded as much, too. She'd told me she wasn't the type of girl who invited men into her hotel room, and I knew, without a doubt, that she was telling the truth. And that I couldn't —

Wait, were the beds moving? Were we in Hogwarts?

She walked in front of me, a blur of beauty and grace while I was a fumbling, drunken fool. I wasn't used to meeting women like this. I didn't always have the advantage, but I definitely had the *dis*advantage this time. Her long, curly blonde hair looked soft and touchable, and I was pretty sure she had bright bluish-hazel eyes that almost matched the blue streak in her hair. Unless I was seeing things.

If only she would stop moving so fast, I might be able to know for sure. And she was on the short side, maybe five foot two, with all the right curves in all the right places. I hated stick-thin women — ironically, that's what Sarah had been—and this woman here was shaped like Christina Hendricks. She was *delicious*.

But I wouldn't touch her.

I'd lied to her earlier. I had noticed the women in the bar, but I'd only really noticed one of them. Her. I'd seen her whispering with her friend, and something had struck home. As if I knew her, someway, somehow, even though I *knew* I didn't. So I'd come up with a lame excuse to talk to her at the elevators. I'd had to see if she was as intoxicating up close as she was far away.

She was even more so.

I stood at the foot of one of the beds, not sure what to do. The two beds swam across the room, blurring into one, and I had no idea if she'd already claimed one as her own. And the whole room smelled like a fruity girly scent. Perfume, maybe.

It smelled good. I kind of wanted to roll around in it and forget all about Sarah and her cheating ways. Forget all about my broken soul.

Forget I wasn't capable of actually feeling love.

Not for someone who would love me back, anyway.

"What's the matter?" She flopped onto a bed—at least I think it was a bed, I couldn't really tell—and rested her head on one hand. "Never seen a hotel room before?"

I squinted. "Not one with beds that moved."

"Oh my God. You're hilarious." She laughed and stood up, coming back over to me. "Let me help you."

Her laugh was perfection. Just like her. What was it about this girl that called to me like this? I'd never felt this strong pull toward another person. Not even the girl I'd once thought I'd loved, Carrie Wallington. Well, Carrie Coram now.

Slowly, she unpeeled my fingers from my briefcase handle and set it down. I closed my eyes. "I wish the room would stop spinning. Are we on one of those towers that revolve to show you the city?"

"I don't think they have one of those here." She smiled up at me. Her face blurred and swam, but she still looked beautiful. "Next time you decide to drink the whole bar, remember this feeling."

She undid my tie, gently pulling it over my head. I let her, even though no one else had ever helped me undress, but I didn't open my eyes. Something about the way she took care of me touched something deep inside me that I didn't even recognize. If I looked at her, it would only make it all the more intimate. "I'll try."

"I'm sorry you had to see, you know, her and him, together like that." Sliding her hands up my shoulders, she slid my suit jacket off with a tender touch. I swallowed hard, my body responding in ways that weren't welcome. Not here and not now. "That must've broken your heart."

"Actually, it didn't." I opened my eyes, staring down into her hazel—yep, they were definitely more blue than green—eyes. "I didn't love her. I was marrying her because I was expected to, and she was nice, and I cared about her, but I didn't love her. Not like I should have."

She cocked her head to the side. "You didn't love her?"

"Nope," I admitted. "I was more upset they were naked on my couch than I was that she was screwing the guy." I paused, blinking a few times. "That's bad, isn't it? It's so bad."

"I don't think so, no. It was probably a nice couch."

"It was." I nodded for good measure, but it hurt my head, so I stopped. "It really was."

She watched me closely, no condescension or judgment showing. "Did she love you?"

"No." I lifted a shoulder. "She loved him. I can't blame her for going to him. Not really. I'm broken. I don't know how to love anyone. Not the right way. I've only ever really loved her."

She pursed her lips. "Her? Who is that, if not your fiancée?"

"Carrie. My best friend." I closed my eyes, picturing her red hair and bright smile. For some reason, the familiar pang of longing didn't hit me. Weird. "I loved her, but she didn't love me. She's the only woman I ever loved."

"Why didn't she love you back?"

"She'd already met her soul mate." I opened my eyes. "He's a great guy, and I'm happy for them. So happy. I'd never interfere between the two of them, not in a million years. They're the only couple I know that's truly in love. Truly happy, like in the movies. But I wish…"

I trailed off, and she nodded, as if I had finished that thought. "I get it."

"How?" I stared at her, trying to see inside those hazel eyes. "Did you love your best friend, too?"

"Yeah." She smiled, but she looked so sad. "I did."

"What happened to him?"

"I married him." She glanced away, swallowing hard. "We were very happy. Too happy. But then…"

I felt her pain more than I felt my own. Maybe I was even drunker than I'd originally thought. "He died."

"Yeah." She turned back to me. For the first time all night, I could see clearly. And I saw her. Really saw her. "He died. He left me."

Reaching out, I cupped her cheek. I might not know her very well, but I felt as if we'd been friends for years. That strange connection I'd felt to her from across the room hadn't shut off. It was probably the drink talking, but this woman affected me in ways I didn't fully understand. I wanted to make her feel better. I wanted to help her. The thing was, though, I didn't know how. "I'm so sorry."

She blinked up at me, her hazel eyes startlingly clear in a world where all the lines were blurred. "I am too."

We stood there, her with her hands on my shoulders, me with my hand on her cheek, and neither one of us moved. "Noelle…"

"Right." Shaking her head, she laughed uneasily and removed her hands. She wasn't done, though. She undid my buttoned collar. "Don't worry, I'm not taking advantage of you. I'm just getting you comfortable so you can sleep."

"If anyone took advantage of the situation, it would be me." I caught her hand. "I'm drunk, and I'm a hot mess, but I don't want you to get the wrong idea about me. I'm not a guy who accepts an act of kindness and then repays it by being a stereotypical jerk."

She blinked. "Who said you were? You've shown no inclination to take advantage of me in any way, shape, or form. I don't blame you for not being interested. You just broke up with your fiancée and you're, well—" She gestured at my stomach. "You're hot. You could have your pick of anyone, so I'd hardly expect you to be falling all over me. I'm extraordinarily ordinary."

I had a hard time keeping up with her fast flow of words in my current state, but I was fairly certain that she'd just put herself down. Insinuated I couldn't possibly be interested in her for her physical attributes. For some reason, that irritated me.

More than my fiancée screwing some other dude on my couch did.

"You're wrong." I still hadn't lowered my hand from her cheek—which would have probably been a hell of a lot more awkward if I was sober—so I ran my thumb over her sharp cheekbones. She had the cheekbones of a Greek goddess. "If sober and not dependent on your kindness, I'd be kissing you right now."

She undid another button. "Is that so?"

Something about the way she said it made me think she didn't believe I wanted her, which was ludicrous. The woman was gorgeous, but something told me she'd been single since her husband died. She needed someone in her life who could show her how beautiful she was. It made me wonder if she was going to wither up and die alone, or if she'd let herself love again.

"Why are you looking at me like that?" she whispered, her hands still on my third button.

"Because you're beautiful," I said in reply, keeping my voice low. "And I like looking at beautiful things. What else is life for, if not that?"

She laughed. "You're drunk, and you totally stole that line from a book, didn't you?"

"Not so drunk that I don't know what's right in front of my face," I said, running my thumb over her cheekbone again. "You, Noelle, are gorgeous. Inside and out. Don't you ever doubt it, or forget it."

Her eyes drifted shut. Warning bells went off in my head. I wasn't supposed to start anything with her, damn it. She'd been kind, and she deserved kindness in return.

That's all I had been trying to do. Be kind.

But then she closed her eyes and lifted up on her toes...and all my good intentions flew out the window. Lowering my head slowly, giving her plenty of time to push me away or turn her head aside, I moved closer until my lips were almost touching hers. "Tell me to stop if you don't want this."

"Riley..." She inhaled a shaky breath, her fists tightening on my shirt. "Don't feel like you have to do this as a thank you."

"I shouldn't be doing this, because you deserve better." I tightened my grip on her and caught her behind her waist, hauling her closer. Her large breasts pushed against my chest, and I groaned. "Never mistake this for what it really is: the greedy actions of a greedy man. I want you. I know I shouldn't take you, but yet..."

"You want to?" she asked, her wet lips begging to be kissed. "I want to, too."

I dropped my forehead to hers. "Why?"

"I don't know," she admitted. She undid another button. "But I do."

"Noelle..."

"I didn't bring you up here for this," she said breathlessly. "I don't mind that it's happening, but I didn't bring you up here to seduce you."

"And I didn't come here to seduce *you*." I brushed my lips across hers, barely touching. "Which is why I should stop."

"Or not."

She tipped her face up, and I kissed her fully, without overthinking it. The second our lips touched, the world as I knew it changed all around me. Yeah, it sounded corny as shit coming from a guy, but it was true.

So fucking *true*.

She fisted my shirt, holding on tight, and I took control of the kiss. Her breathy moan hit me like a punch to the gut, and I knew I'd do anything to hear it again. Move mountains. Wage war. Fight off flying zombie monkeys. *Anything*.

I backed her toward a bed, hoping my vision was slightly improved from earlier. She fell back on it, her arms snaking around my neck. We hit the mattress with a bounce.

*Thank you, depth perception, for not failing me tonight, even if common sense is.* Cupping her face in my hands, I slanted my mouth over hers, slipping my tongue between her sweet lips. She tasted like pink sugar and vanilla, which seemed impossible.

But it was true, and it was addicting.

Urgency came over me, more so than I'd ever felt with Sarah or any other woman, and I ran my hands down her body, tracing her curves. With trembling hands, she undid my shirt the rest of the way. The second her hands touched my bare chest, I was lost.

Or maybe I was found. I wasn't really sure.

Her nails dug into my pecs, and I groaned. The pain almost snapped me into reality, but I fought it. I didn't want to think this through or be logical. I wanted to feel. Touch. Kiss. Forget. It was so much easier.

And so much more dangerous, too.

# chapter
# four

### Noelle

Everything was moving so fast, too fast, but it felt so *right*. Sure, I hadn't been with another man since Roger had died. Or any other man before him, since we'd been high school sweethearts. And I'd never wanted to be with another man, either for one night or more. But tonight?

I don't know. It just felt right.

Maybe it was him. Maybe it was me. Maybe it was the drinks, the room, or the aching loneliness that had faded away the second he'd asked me if I was checking out. But something about him made me forget, for even a second or two, that I was alone.

And that made me feel guilty.

Especially when he was kissing me like this, and my body was responding in ways it had never responded to Roger. I'd loved him with all my heart, and his touch had never failed to arouse me...

But this was different.

Riley slid his hand under my butt, squeezing with the perfect amount of pressure, and I moaned. My cheeks heated because those sounds kept escaping me, but I couldn't help it. He made me this way. His tongue slid over mine, and I kissed him back, trailing my hands down his chest and over his hard abs. There was no doubt he worked out.

Not with a six-pack like his.

He broke the kiss off and nibbled on my earlobe, sending shivers throughout my body. His touch drove me to places I'd never known, and I didn't want to come back. I pushed his shirt down over his arms, and he lifted his upper body to shrug it the rest of the way off. It fell to the floor behind him.

He sat between my legs and looked down at me with crystal clear green eyes. He'd been drunk before, but now he appeared sober. And the look in his eyes made me feel sexy as hell. It made me feel as if he wanted me, and only me, and couldn't wait to have me.

But I was fooling myself.

The man had just found his fiancée having sex with another dude. He'd probably screw anything that batted its eyelashes at him. I knew this meant nothing to him, and it meant nothing to me, too. But it felt…I don't know. Special.

"You okay?" he asked, his square jaw hard.

"Y-Yeah," I said, tracing his abs with my pointer finger. He shivered. "I was just looking at you."

He cocked his head. "Why?"

"Because I like looking at beautiful things," I said, grinning up at him.

"You stole my line," he said, a grin lighting up his face and eyes. He lowered his body over mine and framed my face with his hands. Slowly and seductively, he ran his thumb over my lower lip. It tingled. "I don't know whether to be flattered or angry."

"Be neither." I buried my hands in his hair and tugged playfully, wrapping my legs around his waist. "Instead, be naked."

"As you wish," he whispered, kissing me again.

While he kissed me, he grabbed the hem of my shirt and tugged it up. The kiss broke off long enough for him to pull it over my head with far too much ease. He'd obviously done this more than I had. Something told me when he was single, Riley excelled at one-night stands.

Unlike me.

He tossed the shirt on the floor with his and stared at me. I had the ridiculous urge to cover my breasts with my hands, since my bra was sheer, but that kind of defeated the purpose of removing our clothing. Plus, the modesty was unwelcome. I was trying to be spontaneous and have some fun.

Reaching down, he slid his finger under my bra strap. "Damn, Noelle. You're gorgeous."

My cheeks flushed. "Thank you."

"You must hear that whenever guys remove your shirt, don't you?" He skimmed his fingers over the edge of the cup, teasing goose bumps over my skin. "Because you're so fucking pretty, it almost hurts to look at you."

"I wouldn't know." I swallowed hard and arched my back, loving the way he was touching me. "I've only been with one."

He froze, the muscle in his jaw ticking. "You've only ever been with him?"

"Yeah." I cocked my head. "Was that a bad thing to admit to you? I'm not good at playing coy or acting more sophisticated than I am."

He rested his forehead on mine and let out a shaky breath. "You have no idea how refreshing that is. Or how humbling it is that you want me, after having a love like that in your life. I don't even know what to say, but I...I..."

Without finishing, he kissed me again, his tongue touching mine and sending deep pangs of need scorching through my veins. Gone was the hesitant touches and the slow caresses. He consumed me, his hands drifting over my bra clasp as he made my head spin from his kisses.

Before I knew it, my bra was off.

He continued kissing me, closing his hands over my breasts and rolling his thumbs over the hard peaks. I moaned and arched my back, digging my nails into his shoulders. He made some sexy-as-hell noise and pressed his hips against mine, showing me exactly how much he wanted me right now...in case I'd had any doubts. I had...

But not anymore.

He was huge and hard and driving me insane with want. I wasn't an expert when it came to erections, but I knew one thing. His was larger than any I'd ever seen or felt, in real life or on my computer. Or in romance books. He ended the kiss and nibbled a path down my neck, over my collarbone, and then flicked his tongue over my nipple.

I buried my hands in his hair and closed my eyes. "Oh my God, yes."

When he scraped his teeth over my nipple, biting down with the perfect amount of pressure to send me flying to the skies, I swore I almost came right there. And he hadn't even touched me down *there* yet.

It was ridiculous and intoxicating and oh-so-delicious all at once.

I wanted more. I wanted it all.

His hand slipped between my legs, up my skirt, and then he was cupping my core. I spread my legs wider, not even pretending to have any modesty at this point. I was way too far gone. As soon as he slid my panties to the side and touched my flesh—yeah, I'm almost embarrassed to admit it—but I came explosively.

"Shit," he murmured, withdrawing his hand. "That was fucking hot. I want to make you do that, again and again."

Oh. My. God. I'd finally let loose with a man, and then I'd gone and blown my load before he even did anything to me. This is why I couldn't have nice things.

I buried my face in his shoulder, refusing to look at him. "If by hot, you mean embarrassing, then yes. Yes, it was."

He chuckled, hugging me close. "There's nothing to be embarrassed about. Being unafraid to embrace sex is the sexiest thing in the world. That was sexy as hell."

Hearing him say it like that, I actually believed it.

"Thank you for that," I said, pulling back and looking into his eyes. "You're a pretty amazing guy. You know that, right?"

Something shadowed his eyes, and he shook his head slightly. "I'm not though. Don't think I am. I'm no good. I'm not even capable of loving anyone. I've tried."

"Shh." I cupped his head, pulling him back down. He let me. It hurt my heart that he actually thought there was something wrong with him because he hadn't loved his fiancée who had also not loved him. It didn't mean he was broken or anything. He just hadn't been with the right woman. Easy peasy. "My turn."

I kissed him lightly and shoved his shoulders. My whole body felt relaxed in the aftermath of the incredible orgasm he'd given me with nothing more than a flick of his wrist. He fell backward, and I had him where I wanted him—flat on his back. He fisted his hands at his sides. "What are you doing?"

"Taking care of you."

I knelt between his legs, trailing the tips of my breasts over his fly. He stiffened, his gaze locked on the sight. He was *so* obviously a breast man. Trailing my fingers down his shoulders, over his pecs, and in between the hard line on his abs, I gripped his belt and undid it. He lay there, letting me.

"Don't move." I pulled the belt apart and undid his button. "No touching."

His jaw flexed. "Seriously?"

"Yep. You need this as much as I did." I grinned. "Okay, maybe not quite as badly..."

He gritted his teeth. "You'd be surprised." I nipped the skin right over his pants, and his abs jerked. "Jesus, Noelle."

Grinning, I carefully undid his zipper. The last thing we needed was for something to get accidentally stuck in the zipper. It might dampen the mood.

He lifted his hips, letting me pull his pants down. He wore nothing under his business suit. I didn't know why that was so hot, but it was. His hands twitched at his sides. I knew he wanted to touch, but it was for his own benefit that I didn't let him.

If he touched me, I'd more than likely be lost again, and I'd forget all about my goal of pleasing him. He'd made me come so easily, and so hard, that it was only fair I do the same to him. Crawling up his body, I kissed him, rubbing my breasts against him.

His arms lifted, and I pulled back. "Uh-uh."

"*Noelle.*" He threaded his fingers in my hair, totally not listening to me. "I'm not the type of guy who lies back and lets the woman do all the work. Let me touch you." He nibbled on my lower lip, melting away my resolve to remain in control of myself. "I *need* to touch you."

Well, when he put it like that, how the heck was I supposed to say no?

I nodded, kissing him again. That was all the answer he needed, because his hands started roaming. First, he pulled my hair, bringing a delightful stinging sensation to my scalp. Then slowly—so slowly it nearly killed me—he moved his hands down my bare back, over my hips, and then he cupped my butt while arching his hips.

The sensation of his bare cock against the satin of my panties nearly did me in again. It wasn't until then that a crucial thought occurred to me. I ended the kiss. "Do you have protection?"

"Shit." He closed his eyes. "I don't. I wasn't exactly…I mean, I was engaged up until tonight. I wasn't exactly sleeping around."

The fact that he'd been loyal to her, when he hadn't loved her, told me so much about his character. More than words ever would. Too bad his fiancée hadn't felt the same way about him. She was a fool for letting him go. "We'll improvise."

He cocked a brow. "Do tell."

"I'd rather show you," I whispered, kissing him again.

As I kissed him, I straddled him and rubbed against him, rolling my hips slowly and seductively like a stripper. I'd seen enough movies to know how it was done. Or, at least I hoped I did. If nothing else, he seemed to like it.

He groaned and gripped my hips, his fingers digging into my skin. "*Noelle.*"

Turning his head aside, he broke our mouths apart and positioned me so he could take my nipple between his teeth. Stars swam in front on my eyes, and I gripped his shoulders tight as I rode him. His erection brushed against my already sensitive clit, and I closed my eyes. His hands roamed over my skin, setting fire wherever he touched. My hips moved faster, and he grunted, arching his hips again.

He sucked my nipple harder and released it with a pop while he thrust against me, his cheeks flushing and his chiseled jaw even harder than before. "You're going to kill me," he managed to say, his eyes locked on mine. "Harder. Faster."

I moved faster, and he matched my rhythm perfectly. He might not have been actually having sex with me, but it was still one of the hottest nights of my life, hands down. The man was a charmer, a sweetheart, and a killer in bed. It was so unrealistic I almost wondered if I'd dreamt the whole thing.

But then he slipped his hand between my legs and touched me…

And all thoughts ceased.

"Oh my God," I breathed.

He moved beneath me, each motion sending me closer to the edge. He lifted his hips off the bed, almost sending me flying off the edge, but he held on tightly as he rolled me beneath him. The second he was between my legs, he was moving, thrusting as if he was inside me. And, man, it felt *good*.

His mouth captured mine again, and the second his tongue touched mine, I started the climb up that mountain. He moaned and framed my face with his large hands, his mouth taking everything I gave and then more. When I tightened beneath him, my hands curling into his bare ass, I screamed into his mouth.

He pumped against me once, twice, and then grunted, pulling away so he didn't come on me. Dropping his head on mine, he let out a shaky breath and said, "Holy shit."

I nodded, taking a deep breath. "Yeah. Same."

He pulled back and looked down at me, a tender look in his eyes that I hadn't expected to be there. It took my breath away for the third time that night. He didn't say anything, just stared at me. Funnily enough, words weren't needed.

"Okay?" he asked.

"Okay." Grinning, I motioned to the other bed. "But I think we're sharing that bed tonight."

He looked down at the mess we'd made, grinning sheepishly. "I think that's a good idea. No roommate?"

I'd already told him as much, but he'd obviously forgotten. "No, she got sick at the last minute."

Pushing off me in one solid, fluid motion, he stood beside the bed and stretched. His hard muscles played upon one another, twisting and rolling and looking way too sexy. He didn't have any tattoos on his body, but he didn't need any.

He was just right the way he was.

Since he was naked, nothing was left to the imagination. I'd known he was huge, but seeing him stand beside me, still semi-hard and glistening in the light, was enough to make me want to jump him again. His hair stood up on edge, and I knew why it stood up this time.

Because of *me*.

Because I'd tugged and yanked and touched him everywhere. The knowledge was heady. He turned around — the backside was equally as pleasant as the front, thank you very much — and rolled the comforter back on the second bed.

Coming back to the side of the bed, he bent down and picked me up as if I was nothing. I clung to him, my heart beating fast. After he settled me on the left side of the bed, he slid my skirt down my legs, turned off the light, and curled up behind me.

When he pulled me into his arms, my back to his front, and curled his body around mine, he kissed the top of my head. "Good night, beautiful."

I blinked away tears that threatened to escape. Stupid, unreasonable, unwanted tears. "Good night."

Without another word, he buried his face in my hair and let out a soft snore. Instantly, he was out. Grinning, I shook my head and snuggled in closer. His arms squeezed around my waist, as if he was scared I might leave him.

He was so kind. So tender. If I wasn't careful, he might take more from me than I was prepared to give. The worst part about that…

He wouldn't even know it.

# chapter
# five

## Riley

The next morning, I woke up with a hell of a headache, a naked woman in my bed, and foggy memories of the night before. I remembered almost everything, including my hot as hell not-sex sex with the woman in the bed next to me. I'd been trashed beyond belief, but nothing would make me forget that.

We hadn't even fucked, and it was still one of the best nights of my life.

Probably always would be.

But I'd been drunk, and I'd probably made a fool of myself. What I remembered as hot and fun and free was probably more the equivalent of me dry humping her and grunting like a pansy-assed teenaged boy with his first girl. And I'd done it with *her*, this gorgeous woman asleep in my arms. Her soft curves were highlighted by the sheet that clung to her body, and just looking at her made me hard all over again.

Damn, she was unreal.

Even in her sleep, she looked soft, beautiful, and approachable. Reaching out, I touched a tendril of her long blonde hair. I could see the blue streak peeking out from under her head. It was as curly as I remembered, and yet extremely soft to the touch. I'd never met a woman with hair as curly as hers that was so damn soft. Her eyes were shut, but I remember them being hazel—but more blue than green.

And when she smiled, dimples popped out. Two of them.

She stirred, crinkling her nose up and rubbing it. I glanced at the clock. It was a little after seven, which meant I was due in at work in forty-five minutes, and I didn't even have a change of clothes with me. I'd have to go home. I'd have to see Sarah. For some reason, that didn't fill me with as much dread as I'd thought it might.

Instead, I felt…resigned.

We were over, and it was probably for the best. Maybe I should stop trying to fill any expectations of my parents and accept the fact that I was meant to be alone. Being alone wasn't the worst thing in the world. If you were alone, no one counted on you to do the right thing. You didn't hurt anyone. And no one hurt you.

That sounded like heaven right about now.

Inexplicably, my eyes fell on the woman next to me again. We'd had a one-night stand—did it count as one of those if you didn't fuck? I had no idea—but I didn't want to leave her side. She was in a hotel, so she obviously didn't live close by. Last night was, by nature, dead before it even started. And yet I didn't want to leave her.

What did that even mean?

She rolled over, giving me her back. I stared at her for another second before I slowly got out of the bed. As I crept around the room looking for my clothing, I realized I had no idea what to do after a one-night stand. Hell, I wasn't exactly the type of dude to screw and dash, despite my awful behavior toward Noelle last night.

I didn't do this shit. Should I leave her a *thanks for the fuck, have a nice life* note? Wake her up and kiss her before leaving? Creep out the door while holding my breath before she stirred? That didn't feel right, though. Not after last night.

After I finished getting dressed, I sat down on the bottom of the empty bed, pulled out my phone, and texted my buddy Finn.

*Dude. Did you have one-night stands before Carrie?*

A few seconds passed, and the message showed as read. Then: *Uh… Yeah. Years ago, though. Why?*

*Because I kind of had one, and I have no idea what the hell to do now.*

This time, the message was read instantly. He started replying within seconds. *DUDE. What about Sarah? What the fuck, man?*

Oh. Right. He didn't know. My fingers flew over the screen. *We're no longer engaged. She seemed to think that it was cool to bone another guy… on my couch.*

I barely hit send before he'd read it. *ON YOUR COUCH?*

I grinned. See? He got it. *Yes. I was so pissed.*

*Dude, I'm sorry.*

I flinched. I should feel sadder. I knew that. I was so fucking broken inside. Dead. *Yeah, well…anyway…*

My phone buzzed. *Sneak out, unless you want to see her again?*

*I don't think so.* I looked over at her. She looked so pretty lying there asleep. *Maybe…kind of. Yes.*

*I suggest no. A one-night stand is a one-night stand for a reason. Run.*

I sighed. He was probably right. But still… *Okay.*

My phone buzzed again. *Carrie wants you to call her at lunch.*

I winced even more. Of course Finn had told her already. They had no secrets. Not anymore, anyway. But I didn't want to talk to her about this. Ever. *Yeah. Sure.*

Standing up, I shoved my phone into my pocket. It vibrated, but I ignored it. As I crept to the door, I picked up my jacket and pulled out my wallet. Not able to leave without a word, I dropped a few twenties on the nightstand—since I'd split the room with her for the night, it only felt fair to pay my way—and left my business card.

If she wanted to reach me again, she'd know how.

As I left, I stole one last look at her sleeping face. She looked so damn pretty and filled me with so much peace that I wanted to turn right back around and crawl into bed with her. But I had a meeting at nine, and I smelled like I'd spent the night in a bar.

Real life called, so I left.

As I drove home, if I could even call it that anymore, I braced myself. Though I was doing okay, we'd still ended an engagement last night. There would be announcements and gossip and worst of all? There would be my parents.

I pulled into what used to be my driveway, shut off the ignition, and went to the door. Her car wasn't there, but it was better safe than sorry. I'd gotten enough of a view of them fucking last night. I didn't need to see them on my favorite chair, too.

I rang the bell, waiting a few minutes.

When she didn't answer, I unlocked the door and walked inside. Funny, it didn't feel like home anymore. Maybe it never had. Hell, I'd felt more at home in a hotel room with Noelle last night than I ever had here.

That was pretty fucked up of me. Sarah had been right to run.

I took the stairs two at a time, turning into my room. As soon as I walked in, I froze. Her ex—or not ex anymore—was in my bed, snoring.

And he was wearing *my* fucking robe.

"Seriously?" The man didn't even move. I stalked over to the side of the bed, ripped the covers off him, and grabbed the lapels of my cashmere robe. "*Give it to me.*"

The man jerked awake, his eyes wide and his hands held in a

coward's position. "Dude. What the — ?"

I punched him in the gut, and it felt good. Really fucking good. "Give me my robe, and get the hell out of my house before I call the cops."

The man rolled out of the bed, hopping comically while holding a hand to his stomach. "Look, I'm sorry, but I love her, man."

"Do you love me, too?" I fisted my hands. "Because the way I see it, you're taking everything that's mine. Give me my fucking robe."

"Okay. You're right." He shrugged out of it. Luckily, he wasn't naked under it, or I'd have to burn it. "Here."

Reaching out, I snatched it out of his hand, trying to fight the urge to hit the son of a bitch again. I wasn't even mad, not really. It was just the principle. He took my fiancée, and I accepted that. But that didn't mean he got everything I owned, damn it. "Now get out. I need to collect some things."

He smoothed his hair, nodded once, and left the room. I stood there, silently seething. The man had balls, if nothing else. I could only hope he truly loved Sarah and treated her right. Or this had all been for nothing. Shaking my head, I started my shower and laid out a suit on the bed. While the water warmed up, I threw a few suits into a suitcase, my toiletries I always had at the ready, and a pair of sweats.

Also, my robe.

Because the fucker wasn't going to rub his bare ass all over that, too.

With a few muttered curses, I made quick work of washing up, and then got dressed. When I came down the stairs, the dude was sitting on my couch watching an old episode of *Friends*.

I walked right up to him, set my bag down, and leaned in his face. "Listen to me, fuckwad. I may not have loved Sarah the way she should've been loved, but I care for her. Hear me now, you treat her right, or I will fuck you up." I smoothed his shirt for him and offered him a smile. "Understood, fucker?"

He swallowed hard and nodded. "Y-Yes."

"Good. Tell Sarah I'll call her to make arrangements."

Picking up my bag, I headed for the door. The weight I'd been carrying around on my shoulders for the last…shit, I don't know… eight years or so, disappeared. I felt light and free and happy. For the first time in my adult life, I felt like I could do any —

"How could you, Riley?" my mother asked, her face pale and her Louis Vuitton purse clutched tight in her hands. "How could you do this to us?"

"Mom?" I blinked at her. "Why are you here?"

"Because your fiancée called me last night." She pressed her thin lips together. Her pearls glimmered in the sun, and she wore the same style of sensible pantsuit that she always wore. I think she slept in the damn things. "You broke off the engagement."

Well, Sarah hadn't wasted any time there. "Did she say why?"

"Yes." Her cheeks flushed. "You should be ashamed of yourself."

Wait, what? "Why me?"

She slapped my arm. "How could you cheat on her? The merger made complete sense for our families, and you did that?" She hit me again. "How could you do that to your father? She was perfect for you."

I clenched my jaw. So, Sarah had turned the tables on me and accused me of cheating on her. How delightfully cutthroat of her. She'd probably spread the story far and wide, so I wouldn't stand a chance of setting anyone straight now.

Sure, I could show Mom the half-naked dude on my couch, but she could argue it had happened after my betrayal. Hell, after I'd left Sarah last night, I had spent the night in Noelle's bed. Besides, it wasn't my style. I didn't go around spreading shit about other people, even if it was the truth.

"She wasn't perfect for me," I said, between clenched teeth. "She was perfect for you and Dad."

She gasped. "How dare you."

"How dare I what?" I held my hands out, my luggage still in my hand and my briefcase in the other. "Tell the truth? I didn't love her, and she didn't love me."

"That's not what it sounded like while she was crying on the phone to me last night." She lifted her chin. I knew what that meant. It meant she was prepared to do battle. "I've gotten *dozens* of calls during the course of the last ten hours, all from people calling our family all sorts of horrific things."

Even though I knew she was being dramatic, shame hit me. I might not care what people thought about me, but my parents did. And it wasn't fair that they were suffering because of something Sarah had done. But to besmirch Sarah's name would only make it look as if we were trying to cover our backs. No one would believe it. "I'm sorry, Mom."

She wiped away tears. Tears I had no doubt were real, for once in her life. "How can we go on? It's all they'll be talking about from here to D.C. What will our friends think?"

"Our friends won't give a damn, Mom." I set my luggage down and hugged her. She might be utterly ridiculous at times, but she was my mom. "The Wallingtons won't believe it."

"Should they not?" She pulled back and looked at me, her green eyes wide. She had her blonde hair pulled back in a sensible bun, and her light red lipstick was as immaculate as always. "You didn't do it, did you?"

Shit. I had to let that slip, didn't I? This is what happened when I tried to help people feel better. I got painted as a manwhore, and then turned around and ruined it with a simple word. "Mom…"

"That little hussy." She pushed off me, her hands in fists. "She's the one who strayed, isn't she?"

"It doesn't matter because she apparently already told everyone, anyway." I lifted a shoulder. "No matter what we say, she got there first. It's too late."

She stomped her foot. "Oh, wait till I see her at the club."

"Mom." I laughed uneasily. "It's okay, really. I think it's better this way."

"Me too," she snapped, her eyes blazing with fire. "She never was good enough for you."

I cocked a brow. "Funny, you just said she was perfect for —"

"Forget what I said," she said. "We'll find you someone better. Someone more like Carrie Wallington."

"I'm not ready for that yet."

"You're not." She patted my arm. "But I am. Go off to work, then. We'll talk about some possibilities later. Like you said, it's not as if you loved her. A grieving period isn't necessary. You still need to get married, and I still need to make it happen."

I hesitated, swallowing back my arguments. With her, it wouldn't matter. She wanted to see me married, and she wouldn't stop until I was. Her town car sat in the road, still running. "Are you okay?"

"Of course I am. Don't worry about me." She patted my chest. "I'll be too busy scoping out your next fiancée to get in the way too horribly."

"Mom, I don't —"

She held her finger up. "Enough. Off to work you go."

Shaking my head, I headed for my Rolls-Royce. As I started the ignition, I watched her through my shades. I could practically see the wheels spinning in her head. Wheels that included marriage and trust fund babies and fortunes to be found.

# chapter
## six

### Noelle

Later that afternoon, I sat in the Starbucks with sixty dollars in front of me. The business card Riley had left behind was tucked away safely inside my jeans pocket. All day long, I'd been going over last night in my head. As I'd been sitting in panels with my favorite authors, internally fangirling even though I was *technically* one of them now, all I'd been thinking about was what we'd done.

How we'd met. What he'd made me feel.

Because, I mean, we'd had a glorious night together. One that hadn't actually involved sex, of course, but might as well have. We'd both gotten our rocks off and had a good time. So, why, then, had he felt the need to run out while I was asleep and leave cash on the nightstand with his contact information? There was only one reason that I could come up with in my scattered brain.

He'd thought I was a prostitute.

Either that, or he was so used to hiring them that he'd assumed I'd appreciate the cash payment for services rendered. My cheeks heated at the thought.

Me. A prostitute?

It was utterly ludicrous.

Emily sat beside me and nudged me with her boot. "Dude, enough.

What's with all the cash?"

I picked it up and shoved it in my pocket. "It's nothing."

"Obviously it's something." She set my macchiato down and sat across from me. Her red hair was shoulder length, and she'd done a cute side ponytail today. She narrowed her brown eyes at me, which looked way more adorable than threatening. I always teased her that she was a pixie sprite because she was so small and cute. "Every free moment we've had today, you've pulled out that money and glowered at it. Either you're debating driving to Vegas for some gambling—in which case, I'm *so* in—or something's on your mind. Spit it out."

I sighed. "Fine."

She waited for me to talk, but I didn't know where to begin. She knew, out of all people, how devastated I'd been when I'd lost Roger. She was his sister—or had been. How was I supposed to tell her that I'd met another man, invited him to my room, had almost-sex with him, and then gotten paid for it?

That kind of news would make her...well...I don't know. I still didn't know how *I* felt about it. I was still trying to figure it out. "Well..."

Sighing, she sat back against the chair and fidgeted. She always did that when she was impatient. So had Roger. "Are you going to tell me what's going on, or am I supposed to read your mind?"

I swallowed. "Remember that guy last night?"

"Which one?"

"The one we saw at the bar, who we didn't know?"

She set her cup down. "Yeah..."

"Well, I ran into him at the elevator. He was drunk, sad, and alone."

Emily narrowed her eyes again. Her freckles across her nose danced as she crinkled it. I couldn't tell how she was taking the news so far because she was so freaking good at hiding her feelings. "Okay..."

"He didn't have a room."

Emily's cheeks flushed. "Oh my God. You didn't?"

"I did." I dropped my head, focusing on the money in my hands. "I invited him to share mine."

"Noelle! You don't even know him!" Emily said, leaning forward. "What if he was a serial killer or a rapist or some other horrible thing I can't think of right now?"

"I considered all those possibilities but rejected them." I lifted a shoulder and glanced at her again. Her mouth was pinched tight, and she gripped the table edge with white knuckles. "He was so nice. I knew I could trust him. Don't ask how, I just...did."

She didn't say anything to that, but she watched me closely. Too closely. "What did he say? Did he come up?"

"Yes." I took a sip of my coffee. Emily practically vibrated with impatience for me to continue. And she fidgeted again. "He came up. And turns out, he's local, and he found his fiancée in bed with another guy. Well, technically, they were on his couch."

"No shit," Emily said, slapping her knee. "He didn't."

"He did," I said, grinning at her reaction. Emily never did anything half-assed. She was always all in. I'd always wished I was a little more like her. Last night, I had been. "So he came to my room and we...did things."

Emily sobered. "You did?"

"Yeah...I'm sorry."

Emily's eyes widened, and she looked so sad it hurt. Shaking her head, she reached out and grabbed my hand. "No. Don't apologize. I mean, it's sad to see you moving on, but not in that way. I don't want you to feel bad, or not to do it. He's dead, Noelle. You shouldn't have to be alone for the rest of your life. None of us should be. But still..." She shrugged. "It's sad, you know?"

"I know." I squeezed her hand back. She gave me a small smile in reply. "But you know how much I loved—*love*—your brother. My whole life, it's always been him. I thought it always would be, but then..."

"He died," Emily whispered. "And it was awful and unfair and too soon." We sat there silently, neither one of us speaking. After a few seconds, she rolled her shoulders and smiled. "But we're still here. Or so I keep telling myself. He'd want us to live. Laugh. Have fun."

I blinked away the threatening tears. "I know."

"So, enough of that sad stuff." Emily let go of me and sat up straight, forcing a smile. To anyone else, she would have looked perfectly happy. But I knew differently. She might be hard to read, but I knew she was dying inside at this conversation. So was I. "So, how was he? Tell me all the smutty details, and leave nothing out. Pretend it's one of your books."

"We don't—" I glanced away, my cheeks hot. "We don't have to do this."

"Hey, it's been more than a year and a half. And I was *your* best friend before he was *your* husband." She smiled brightly, but her hold on the coffee cup was too tight. "So, yeah, we do. How was it? That man was sex on a stick."

I rolled my eyes. "How that phrase ever made sense to anyone, I'll never know. And I'll never use it in a book. If I do, take away my computer."

"Because it does."

"But anyway, we didn't actually do that." I waved a hand in front of my hot cheeks. "We just...kinda...dry humped."

Emily choked on her coffee, arms flying out to the sides. As she flailed dramatically, I grinned and slapped her back for her. She smacked my hand away, swiped her hand over her mouth, then said, "What are you two, fourteen? Oh my God. Tell me *everything*."

So I did. And then I finished it off with, "And he made me feel so... so..."

"Alive?" Emily smiled sadly and nodded once. "You need that. You've been grieving for too long now. Roger would have wanted you to move on."

I blinked and glanced away, an overwhelming sadness hitting me. I'd loved Roger with all my heart, and when he died, a piece of me had died, too. I existed, but not really here. But last night...she was right. I had felt *alive*. It had been amazing.

"I miss him," I whispered.

"I do too." Emily leaned back on her chair again and sighed. "But he's gone. He would have wanted us to keep living. Including dry humping strangers in hotels."

I laughed. "Oh my God."

"Hey, you did it. Not me." Emily flipped her bangs out of her face. "Was he still there when you woke up?"

"No. He'd left his business card, and..." I pointed to my pocket. "Sixty bucks."

Her jaw dropped. "He didn't?"

"Yeah." I nodded slowly. "He did."

"What the *hell*?"

"I don't know." I played with the straw of my macchiato. "I have no idea if he thought I was a, well, you *know*, or if he was just being nice."

"Men aren't supposed to leave cash on the nightstand after a one-night stand." Emily shook her head, her eyes focused on something I couldn't see. "You have to go to him and give it back."

"No." I shook my head. "I couldn't. I can't see him again. No way."

"You have to." She stood up and pulled me to my feet. "It's perfect. March into his office, give him his money back, and say something sassy."

"Like what?"

"I don't know, but we'll think of something." She pulled me behind her. "Get that card out. We're getting a cab."

Twenty minutes later, I walked into the opulent office, not sure why

I'd thought this was a good idea when Emily had suggested it. I tugged on my long tank top and smoothed my hands over my well-worn jeans, feeling more out of place than a hooker in church on Easter morning.

Maybe a lot less welcome, too.

Everywhere I walked, people stared.

While I might like to think it was due to my fabulous hair day and the red lipstick I dared to put on today, paired with my smoky eyeshadow that I redid three times because my hands had been shaking, I knew better.

It was because in a room full of Chanel and Gucci, I was wearing Old Navy. There was no shame in that, and I refused to pretend there was, but to them, I was a peasant. Someone who didn't belong, and they didn't bother to try to pretend otherwise.

"I can't do this. Let's go and—" I broke off when Emily glowered and pushed me forward, and I stumbled up against a huge oak desk that said *reception* on it. "Uh, hello."

The snobby receptionist looked me up and down, her upper lip curled. "Can I help you?"

"It's 'may.' *May* I help you."

The receptionist narrowed her icy blue eyes at me. "*May* I help you?"

"I need to speak to Mr. Stapleton." Lifting my chin, I set down Riley's card. "Please."

She pushed the card back to me with one finger, as if scared it might be diseased. "He's not available for social calls. You need to schedule an appointment."

Emily huffed behind me. "Tell him she's here, Miss Priss."

"I will not." She stood up to her full height of five foot three. In heels. "We have protocol, and we don't let people just walk in to speak to him unannounced."

Geez, I'd had no idea Riley was so freaking important that he needed advance warning of visitors. What the heck, man? I raised my brows and took my cell out. Important man or not…this skinny little bitch was going down.

Slowly and deliberately, I dialed. "We'll see what he says about that type of treatment. I mean, he told me to be here at five o'clock sharp, and I am, but his secretary won't let me come back to see him. He won't be pleased."

Blondie paled a little bit. "*Wait.*"

"Yes?" I hovered with my finger over the dial button. I had no idea if he'd actually answer or give a crap that I was being held back from his office, but I'd been prepared to find out the hard way. "What is it?"

"I'll check with him. What's your name again?"

"Noelle Brandt." I smiled and tucked my phone back into my back pocket. "I'll wait right here."

Blondie scowled at me, then pushed a button on the phone. Within seconds, she said, "I have a Noelle Brandt here to see you, sir. She says you're expecting her."

I watched closely, dying to know if he'd play along and let me in his office that I could *see* from here, or if he'd pretend he wasn't there. Blondie hung up, looking like she'd swallowed a crow whole. Guess I got my answer. "He's ready for you."

"Should I show myself back, or do I need to be escorted?"

"Last door at the end of the hallway." She motioned me forward. "You can — *may* go alone."

I smiled and winked at Emily. "Thank you."

Emily grinned. "Go on. I'll wait here with our new best friend."

"But — "

"You have to do this alone." She pushed me again. "Go. Be sassy."

I swallowed hard and walked to his door, my heart beating faster with each step I took. Why had I let Emily talk me into this? Damn her and her bold —

The door swung open and Riley was there. *Smiling* at me.

Damn, he looked even hotter sober than he had drunk. How was that fair? His blond hair wasn't sticking up anymore, and he had another expensive suit on. Obviously, because he was a lawyer. From the looks of it, a lucrative one. *Duh.*

"Noelle." He opened the door wider, gesturing me inside. Part of me had expected him to be a complete jerk sober. But nope. He seemed as kind as ever. "I'm so happy you came to see me. I'd hoped you would."

I took a deep breath and walked into his office, stealing one last look at Emily as I did so. She made an "oh my God" face and fanned her cheeks. Obviously giving her approval. Yeah, most women still alive would. Maybe even the dead ones would perk up if Riley Stapleton walked by their graves.

"Hi," I managed to say, feeling as if I was tripping all over my tongue in his presence. "It's...uh...I..."

He closed the door behind him and leaned on it, crossing his arms. "I think I know why you're here. I'm sorry about last night. I was out of line."

That spurred me into action. Up until I woke up to find a payment on the nightstand, it had been the sexiest night of my life in *waaaaay* too long. I didn't want him apologizing for it. That would cheapen the night we'd shared.

And why was I being all tongue-tied now? This was the same Riley

I'd been with last night. There was no reason to be nervous or shy. None at all. Crossing my arms, I gave him the stink eye. "That's not what you should apologize for."

He blinked. "It isn't?"

"Nope. Try again."

"You're upset I left? Truth be told, I've never really—"

"Try again."

He pushed off the door, his jaw hard. "I'm fresh out of ideas. Why don't you tell me, so I can apologize for it again?"

"This." Reaching into my pocket, I pulled out the sixty bucks and slammed it down on his desk. "You didn't leave me enough."

"What?" He stopped mid-stride, his eyes on the money.

I stalked toward him. "How dare you pay me for—?"

At the same time, he held his hands up and said, "I'm sorry, I don't understand. Did I not cover my half of the room?"

"No, you didn't—" I stopped walking. "Excuse me?"

He reached into his pocket. "If you need more money for my half of the room, just tell me how much. I'm sorry if I underestimated."

"That's why you left money on the nightstand?"

"Yeah." His fingers hovered over his wallet. "Why else would I...?" His face turned red. "Oh, *shit*. No. No, no, no."

"Uh-huh." I hugged myself and looked away from him, the heat filling my cheeks and spreading down my chest. "I thought you thought I was a...you know. A hooker."

He shook his head. "Jesus. No. Never. I'm so sorry, Noelle."

"I see that you're accustomed to the type of lifestyle that accommodates that kind of thing." I broke off and gestured around the office.

Everything in it screamed of money. I'd known he wasn't poor from his suit last night, but man, I hadn't realized he was *loaded*. Truth be told, I didn't like that.

"Jesus, Noelle, I don't hire hookers," he said, his face even redder.

"I don't do this, what we did together last night, and to wake up to find a bunch of cash by the bed...it hurt. I'd thought we'd connected, but then I thought that you thought—" I stopped talking. I was babbling now, and he didn't say a word. He just kept staring at me, seemingly speechless. "Anyway. Keep your money. I don't want it. I only wanted to help. I hope things are better today. So...uh...bye."

"Wait." He crossed the distance between us. Gently, he grasped my chin and lifted it up. When I met his eyes, his soft green ones were tender and kind. Just like him. How could I have ever thought he'd meant to insult me? I should have known better. "I would never have thought you were a prostitute. I know why you invited me up, and I was trying to repay that kindness through a gesture of paying my way. In retrospect, maybe leaving money by the side of the bed was a bad idea."

I snorted. "You think?"

"But, in my defense?" He brushed his finger over my jaw. "I've never had a one-night stand. I had no idea what to do or say, so I kind of panicked."

My heart melted. "You haven't?"

"If I had, do you think I'd have been dumb enough to leave money by the bed?" Laughing, he rested his forehead on mine. "Last night was amazing. I'm only sorry I was drunk like that. What I remember as sexy moves on my part were probably awful."

I gripped his suit lapels. "Up until the money thing, you had me hooked."

"Ugh." Pulling back, he pressed his lips to my temple. "Any chance of me reclaiming that spot?"

"Hmm...I don't know." I lifted my face to his. His eyes sparkled and drew me in. Reaching out, I ruffled his blond hair. "That's a little better."

Grinning, he yanked at his tie, loosening it so he looked sloppily put together. It was more attractive than it should have been. "Even better?"

"Mmhmm." I skimmed my fingers over his shoulders. "So...a lawyer, huh? A rich one, at that?"

"Yep," he said, looking at me sheepishly. "You look horrified at the thought. Most girls like both of those labels."

"I'm not most girls."

His fingers flexed on me. "I'd noticed that."

"I just hadn't pegged you for a lawyer. They're so..." I tugged at his tie a little more. "Uptight."

He backed me toward the wall, his steps predatory. "Is that so?"

"Mmhmm." I hit the wall and splayed my hands out on either side of my hips, trapped by his hard body and loving it. "They certainly wouldn't have done dirty things to me in my hotel room."

"Ah, but this lawyer did. I did." He pressed his body against me, slipping his leg between mine. I moaned when his knee brushed my clit. God, I was already horny as heck and he hadn't even really done anything. It was ridiculous. "And I'd like to do it again, only for real this time."

I closed my eyes. "Would you?"

"And I won't leave money behind this time, unless you don't mind now that you know it's not a payment?" He kissed my jaw. "I'd like to help pay for the room. It's only fair."

That ruined the moment for me. I turned my face away from his. "I don't want your money. Every other girl in your life might have wanted to get her grubby hands on it, but I'm not one of them."

I had my own money, thank you very much.

"Fine." He nibbled on my throat, making my pulse skyrocket. "Can I stop by later, though?"

My heart raced right out of my chest. "Why? Do you have nowhere to go again?"

"I'm not going home, but I could get a hotel room of my own." He slipped his fingers between my legs slowly, giving me a chance to push him away, no doubt. I'd sooner rip my arm off and eat it. "But it wouldn't have a hot little blonde with a blue streak in her hair just waiting for me..."

"Hot, huh?" My pulse skyrocketed even more. "And I'm not little."

"You're little," he said, nibbling on my ear. I arched my neck for him. "But you're curved in all the right places. It's addicting, Noelle. All day long, all I could think about was you. Your laugh. Your voice. The way you let me in last night, out of the kindness of your heart. Your smile. How good your hair smells." He inhaled deeply, letting off a soft groan. As he talked, his fingers moved over me, sure and steady. "The way you let out a breathy little moan when you come..."

"Oh my God, *Riley*."

"Mm." His fingers moved faster. "Close, but not quite. Go ahead. Sing for me, angel."

I ran my hands over his arms, admiring how hard and big they were. What kind of lawyer was built like this? "I can't. Someone might hear."

"I don't give a damn who hears." He pressed even closer, dominating me. Taking control. The man was a completely different lover while sober. It was intoxicating. "You have no idea how close I am to fucking you right here, against my door."

"Oh my God."

Yeah, that's the best I had in the face of his dirty talking.

His free hand rolled over my left nipple, squeezing with the right amount of pressure to hurt just a little bit. "Come for me, Noelle. I need to hear that moan again."

The tension built higher and higher. He was wearing a suit, and we were in his office, and I could hear people walking by. Hell, my sister-in-law was outside waiting for me. But knowing all of that only made it even hotter. Tossing my head back, I rolled my hips and moaned, my stomach tightening with each motion of his fingers.

"Yes. Fuck, yes." He bit down on my shoulder. "*Noelle*."

Crying out, I closed my eyes and colorful stars exploded in my vision, making me collapse against the wall. His fingers stopped moving, but he didn't take them away. That somehow made what we'd just done even hotter than before.

Once I managed to gather my breath, I had one thing to say. "When will you be by my room?"

Grinning, he pulled back and gazed down my body with hungry eyes. "Eight sound good? I have a meeting, but then I'm free."

Nodding quickly, I smoothed my shirt over my fluttering stomach. "I'll be there?"

"Was that a question?"

I laughed. "Uh, maybe?"

"You're too much." He tapped underneath my chin, his gaze possessive and dominant and hot. "Just so you know, all throughout my meeting, I'll be thinking of the best way to make you make that sound again. I'll be expecting you to be ready for me."

My stomach twisted and turned, and my panties got even wetter than they already were—which was saying a heck of a lot. "Don't forget the condoms this time."

"Oh, I won't," he promised.

Tossing him a cocky look, I strutted out of his office, swinging my hips with each step I took. "Oh, and when you're at those meetings, think of what I'm doing to myself while I'm waiting for you."

He let out a strangled groan. "Holy shit."

Grinning, I wiggled my fingers in a little wave and shut the door in his face. "See ya on the flip side."

"*Noelle*," he growled.

Strangled curses came from the other side of the door, and I laughed. Flipping my hair over my shoulder, I walked right past Blondie and caught Emily's hand as I walked by her. She'd been chatting with some handsome man in a suit but didn't seem to mind the abrupt exit. "Were you sassy?"

"Oh yeah."

Emily eyed my hair and skimmed her gaze over my clothes. Knowledge lit her eyes, and she smirked. "Is he coming over tonight?"

"Oh yeah," I repeated, grinning.

# chapter
# seven

### Riley

Pulling into the parking spot in front of Food Lion, I shut off my car and leaned back in my seat. Without moving, I listened to my client as he babbled on and on about his company's investments and 401(k) issues. And I was bored out of my mind.

I'd never wanted to be in law. It had never been my calling. But the one time I'd hinted I might like to do something else, my mother had fallen into a fit of vapors, and my father had lectured me throughout the night about what it meant to be a Stapleton.

Sometimes I wished I wasn't one.

Life would be so much easier.

"And then we can consolidate it all, and maybe we can close out the accounts in the black," my client said in a rush. "Do you think it'll work?"

I pinched the bridge of my nose. "It's certainly possible, sir. But that's something you'll have to run across your accounting firm. I'm only a lawyer, not a CPA."

"Right." He cleared his throat. "Sorry, I got carried away there for a second."

"Don't worry, sir. It's what I'm here for." Not really. "To be your sounding board."

I could practically hear his chest puff out over the phone. "Indeed."

"So, why don't you run that by your board and let me know how it goes?" I sighed. "I'm headed out of the office now, but I'll keep my phone on in case of any emergencies."

"Great. Oh, and before I hang up, did I tell you about my latest golf score? The other day with your father I got—"

As he spoke, I tuned him out and watched the young couple walking out of the store. They were all smiles and handholding, and something the young man said made the woman crack up. When she laughed, her boyfriend pulled her close and grinned even wider, seemingly proud of the fact that he'd made her smile.

They looked so happy and free.

What did that feel like? To be able to do anything you might like and not give a damn about anyone else's reactions? It's something I'd never known.

And probably never would.

The closest I'd gotten was Noelle. She was someone my mother would never approve of, not in a million years. But she made me happy, and I liked her.

So, for now, I didn't give a damn.

I'd spent my whole life doing my best to be a proper Stapleton. I'd spent so long trying to be what everyone expected of me, I wasn't really sure who "I" was anymore.

Or who I wanted to be.

"—and then I got a hole in one!"

"That's excellent, sir," I managed to say with some small amount of excitement for his benefit. "But you better get going. It's almost six, so your accounting team will be leaving soon."

After some hurried goodbyes, I hung up and dropped the phone on my lap. I don't know what it was that had changed, but suddenly, I felt as if I was drowning.

I didn't want to be the guy I'd become. As a kid in college, I'd been so sure I would grow up independent of the values my parents had tried to stuff down my throat. When I'd met Carrie, we'd both laughed and sworn we'd never be like our parents.

And I'd been so sure we were right.

But then when I'd been twenty-five, my father had suffered from a stroke, and for a few days, we hadn't been sure if he'd survive. And in those few days, I'd become a different man. My mother had needed me to be a true Stapleton, and I'd slipped into that mold way too fucking easily.

I'd never gotten out of it.

Before I'd fully realized what was going on, I'd agreed to date the type of women I was expected to date, and I'd been working at my father's old law firm, and I hadn't even recognized who I'd become. I didn't think I ever really would.

My phone buzzed in my lap again, and I muttered a few curses. Lifting it to my ear, I said, "Riley Stapleton. How can I help you?"

"It's me," Carrie said, her voice tinged with amusement. "God, for a second there, you sounded like your father."

I dropped the professional act, but her words hit home worse than usual. She was right. I had sounded like him. Hell, I'd become him, and I hadn't even realized it. "Screw you. You sounded like your mother."

She gasped. "Damn, Riley. That's low."

"Just like my father," I said, grinning. "I was playing the part."

"You've been playing it a little bit too well, if you ask me," Carrie muttered. "Where are you? Drop everything and come over to my place. We're having lasagna."

My stomach growled. If they were having lasagna, then Finn was cooking it. And he made a damn fine lasagna. "I can't."

"Why not? Working late *again*?"

I flinched. The past three times she'd invited me over, I'd been too busy working. In fact, it had to have been more times than that. When had I let work and family duty overrun my entire life? When had I become my father? "Actually, not tonight."

"Oh?" Carrie paused. "What are you doing? Do you have to meet up with Sarah?"

A young family came out of the store. The mother and father swung a toddler in the air, and her infectious laughter filled the air. Again, the sight hit me hard. Like a fist to the gut, or a kick to the nuts. I was missing so much in my life.

I'd thought, for a second, that I might get some of this stuff with Sarah. The family. The laughter. The love, eventually. Maybe. But then it had all gone away, and suddenly, none of that felt like enough. None of it felt real.

What had changed in my life?

I'd met Noelle. That was it.

"No, I'm just busy." I cleared my throat, forcing my eyes off the young family, and turned my car off. I should get out and go inside, but I didn't move. Carrie was a therapist, so she was good at helping people. I'd never gone to her for help, because I'd never felt like I'd needed it, but tonight I did. "Hey, did you ever wonder how we become what we are? What led us here?"

Carrie was silent for a minute, and I almost took my question back. It sounded stupid, and I was stupid, and—

"Of course. I think the best way to answer that is this: I believe that every choice we make, we leave behind a whole life, basically."

I scrunched my forehead. "Uh, what?"

"Think about it. You're outside a store, and you're deciding what you want for dinner." I actually *was*, but I kept that to myself. "You're going inside, and you see a woman who takes your breath away. You can't stop looking at her, even though you never met her. She looked different from what you're used to, a little wild and free, and you like that."

Sounded like how I'd felt with Noelle last night. Something about her had called to me, and I'd been unable to look away. Unable to resist. Actually, it sounded as if Carrie described Noelle perfectly, as if she knew. "Okay…"

"You have two choices right then. Go up and talk to her, or walk by and go inside the store. Say you go inside the store. You never get to know her. You might meet someone else inside the store, someone sensible and just your type, and you might hit it off with her. But that one woman outside the store? What about that whole life you might have had if you went up to her, said hello, and got her number?"

I swallowed and tightened my grip on the phone. "That woman might be a killer, married, or a democrat." I'd added that last one for her amusement.

"That's true." Carrie paused. "But then again, she just might have been the woman in your dreams. But it doesn't matter, because if you didn't go up to her, then you'll never find out. It's a whole other life you'll never actually live."

"But you could be perfectly happy with the sensible woman you met in the store. The sensible one your parents would like, that would fit in with your life, and bear you wonderful children."

"You could." Carrie laughed. "But then, what would life have been like with the woman who stole your breath away? Would it have been wild and free and *fun*?"

I rolled my eyes, even though everything she said made complete sense. And now, more than ever, I was determined to spend time with Noelle while I could. To have fun, be free, and not give a damn if she'd fit in my lifestyle. It didn't matter. "You basically just described what life would have been like if you married me versus Finn. You know that, right?"

She sighed, and it was heavy with regret and affection and God only knew what else. "Sorry. I didn't—"

"There's nothing to be sorry for. You went up to that girl outside the store—metaphorically speaking. And don't you ever tell Finn I called him a chick."

Carrie laughed again, the regret gone from her voice. Thank God. I didn't want her to feel bad for making the choice to live for herself. In a way, I wished I could be her. "I did go up to him. And I took the chance on a guy who didn't fit the mold."

"I used to think I'd do that, too. But now..." I thought of Noelle and her sparkling hazel eyes and light blonde hair with a touch of blue in it. "I'm not so sure."

"I like to think you would. The Riley I met, when we were young? He would have." She hesitated. "You've changed, there's no hiding it. But that doesn't mean you can't change again."

"I've changed for the worse. I've become a *Stapleton*."

"You were always a Stapleton, even when you weren't," she said, her voice soft. "You're still you. If you met the right girl, and you fell for her...I bet you'd do anything to keep her. To have her. It's just... Sarah wasn't that girl."

I closed my eyes, shutting out the real world. Sarah had never been, and never would be, that girl. But Noelle...

I liked Noelle. I liked her a lot. I'd already gone up to her and gotten the introduction. I hadn't walked away. I'd gone up to her room, and we'd had an amazing night. And then, despite the idiotic move on my part with the cash I'd left behind, she'd agreed to see me again. I'd already taken that leap. I'd already said hello. I'd already chosen the insensible choice, and it had felt amazing.

And something told me, deep down, if I wasn't too much of a pussy, and if I really opened myself up to her, and all the things we could be...

She could *be* that girl.

# chapter eight

## Noelle

I sat up on the erotic writers panel, staring out at the crowd that had filed into the room forty-five minutes ago. We had a full house, which rocked, and we even had some people standing against the back wall so they could listen in.

But I *sucked* at these types of things. Give me a pen and a piece of paper, and I could write the most eloquent sentence you'd ever read. My fingers would fly over the keyboard, and I'd have hit a thousand words in less than an hour. But put me behind a mic with a bunch of eyes on me, expecting me to drop some magical pearls of wisdom that would make them smile?

And I closed up like a clam.

We'd spent the last forty-five minutes talking about writing hot scenes and how to keep readers sucked into the books. But now it was time for the Q&A portion of the panel. I leaned back in my folding chair, figuring I'd have time to zone out now. There were six authors on this panel, the others being more popular than me, so it made perfect sense that no one would have a question for me.

Now I could think about Riley, and why he was so darn irresistible, and what it all meant. Heck, all my life I'd lived very sensibly. Yes, I had blue in my hair, and I wrote steamy books with happy endings—

pun intended — but when push came to shove I was hella boring.

I didn't take risks on people, and I didn't act out without first thinking of every possible effect from my actions. After being raised by my parents, I hadn't had a choice.

There was no way I was going to make the same mistakes they had. No way I'd ever act without thinking and make rash decisions, no matter how small.

But then I'd met Riley, and I'd invited him up to my room. I'd broken every rule I'd lived by since my parents had gone away. Every strict, decisive, thorough rule had been broken in an instant, and all for a tall blond guy with green eyes and a devastating smile. I'd been a different woman for him.

And it had felt so *good*.

A red-haired woman in the front row raised her hand, and our moderator pointed at her. I vaguely recognized her as one of my readers. "Yes, you, in the front."

"My question is for K.M."

I perked up, forcing my mind off Riley. Anything that took my mind off him was probably a good thing. I'd become borderline obsessed with that man and how he made me feel. "Uh, yes?"

"You were widowed recently, correct?"

Stiffening, I leaned closer to the microphone. I'd been wrong. Anything that took my mind off Riley would not be better. "Yes, but —"

"Don't worry, I'm not going to ask what happened or anything," she said quickly, shooting me an apologetic smile. "I was just wondering if it's hard for you to write happy endings sometimes, because you were so tragically robbed of your own."

Emily glanced at the woman with wide eyes, her cheeks pale. I knew the question upset her, but there was no avoiding it. Almost every time, someone asked me this. Most of the time I gave a half-assed answer and avoided the question. But this time...

"No. It's not hard at all. I think despite tragedy and heartbreak and pain...everyone gets their happy ending." I saw Emily turn to me slowly, her eyes locked on me. I didn't meet her eyes. "It might take longer, and it might be riddled with tears and blood and disappointment, but who says a widow can't have a happy ending, too? For now, I get mine through my characters. But, God, I hope I get my own happy ending someday. I don't want to live my life alone."

As soon as the words left my mouth, I sank against the chair again. Really, I couldn't believe I'd said them. For the longest time, I'd never even thought about a life with someone besides Roger. He'd been the man I loved my whole life.

How could I ever love again?

But even though I was shocked I'd said them, I knew they were true. I did want a happy ending eventually. And it couldn't be with Roger, because he was dead.

I loved him and missed him, but it was true.

He'd died, and I hadn't.

Emily clapped, and the whole room joined her. My cheeks flushed, and I shook my head, locking eyes with her. She nodded once, and she looked happy for me. For a while now, she'd been telling me that exact thing, but I'd refused to admit that one day I might love again. That I might open myself up to someone.

But now, suddenly, I was ready. I'd be a fool to not see why: Riley. Something about him had awakened that part inside me that yearned for a happy ending. I'd had a hard life filled with murders and hatred and a tiny bit of love. Was it so bad to want some more of the latter? The guilt I felt said so.

Someone else asked another panelist a question, and I zoned out for the rest of the panel. By the time it was over, I was numb. One night in Riley's arms, and I was ready to move on? Forget about Roger and what he'd meant to me?

He'd been the one staple in my life. Him and Emily.

Now he was gone.

Emily came up to me and hugged me. When she pulled back, her forehead scrunched up and she frowned. "Hey, don't do that."

"What?" I asked, glancing around the room. It had emptied out, minus a few stragglers who were grouped in the back staring at the schedule. "What am I doing?"

"Backtracking." She stepped back and crossed her arms, nibbling on her lower lip. "You said you want a happy ending, and now you feel bad about it."

I swallowed hard and made a tiny tear in my name tag they'd placed in front of me for the panel. "Do you blame me? It...it's not right."

"Shut up," Emily said, tearing the paper out of my hands. She chucked it into the garbage can and whirled on me, anger shining in her dark eyes. "I'm so sick of this."

Blinking at her, I stumbled back a step. "Of what?"

"You acting like you died, too. He was my brother. Believe me, I know how special he was. How wonderful he was." Emily sat down heavily, staring at the wall blankly. "I miss him, too. But if you can't move on and be happy, how will I ever be able to? You have to move on, damn it. And so do I."

Tears blurred my vision, and I sat down beside her. Gently, I put my arm around her and hugged her close. "Your happiness doesn't have to be tied to mine. If I'm not ready to move on, then that doesn't mean you can't be."

"But it does." She swiped her hands over her cheeks angrily. Emily hated crying, and she considered it a sign of weakness. "If you can't be happy without him, how can I be? Seeing you so sad and alone only reminds me how much he left behind. How much he missed out on, and how much you'll miss out on, too. You can't be scared to grab on to your next happy ending, damn it, just because you lost your first one."

For some reason, Riley popped in my mind. Could he be my happy ending? I shook my head. Of course not. He was a fling. He lived here, and I lived across the country. And on top of that, we'd never once talked about anything serious.

I liked him because he made me feel alive—made me forget, even for a second—who I was and what I'd lost. Made me forget that everyone I loved left me, in one way or another. My parents had left me through a sequence of horrible, terrible, bad decisions, and Roger had left me because someone else had made horrible decisions, and ripped his life away from him...and me.

It was an equation that had only one constant. *Me.*

"I'm not afraid to grab on to a happy ending. If I found one, I'd take it," I said defensively.

"So if this Riley guy wanted more than what you were ready to give him," Emily said, drying her cheeks off one more time. All signs of tears were gone. "You'd let him in? Let yourself care?"

I hesitated. "Uh..."

"See?" She punched me in the shoulder. "You're not ready to move on."

"But I am." I stood up and paced, nibbling on my thumbnail. "I think I am. I mean, I let him in my room and...did things. Lots of things. And he's coming back in an hour. That means something, right?"

"It does. Of course it does." Emily snagged my hand and tugged me so I sat beside her. Once I was seated, she grabbed my other hand. "But I want you to promise me something."

I nodded. "Anything. You know that."

"If you feel like maybe, just maybe, Riley could make you happy." She swallowed hard. "As happy as Roger made you, or even happier—"

I pressed my lips together. "Emily, no. He was the best thing to happen to me, and that will be forever true. No one—"

"Could make you happier than him. I know you think that, but it might not stand true." She smiled at me, but her eyes seemed sad. Resigned, but sad. "Forever is a long time. But promise me that if you meet a guy who could make you happy, whether or not it's Riley, that you give him a shot. Don't shut him out. Roger would want that for you, and I do, too."

I stared at the empty room. It was much like my life lately. I wrote books in my pajamas, never went out, and my only friends besides Emily were on Twitter. Empty things. Emptiness. "Fine. I will. But only if you promise to do the same. When's the last time you went out on a date?"

She flinched. "The last time I was with a man was the night Roger died. I kind of…" She twisted her lips. "Associated it with that, I think. So now, I don't want to revisit that night. Stupid, right?"

I shook my head. "Not stupid at all. Feelings are never stupid, no matter how much it might feel like it at one point or another."

"Yeah. But anyway, I promise, too." She let go of me and held her pinky up. "I hereby pinky promise to open my heart to a man, if I find one that awakens my lady parts without stirring up any residual guilt."

Grinning, I locked pinkies with her. "And I hereby pinky promise to do the same, whether it's Riley or some guy back home…which would make more sense than Riley."

"Since when did the heart *ever* make sense?" Emily asked, cocking a brow.

Laughing, we shook pinkies.

The deal was on.

# chapter
# nine

## Riley

A little before eight o'clock at night, I walked into the crowded hotel bar for the second night in a row, my hands full with bags and boxes. After a few steps, I stopped and blinked. The place was filled with women, all laughing and chatting and drinking. Had it been this crowded last night?

All I remembered was Noelle, sitting there sipping her wine. If it had been this packed, how had I missed it? Oh. Right.

Whiskey and disillusionment could be a bitch.

"Riley?"

I stopped. A short redheaded woman stood in front of me. She had rich brown eyes, cute freckles, and was extremely pretty. I knew, without asking, that this was Noelle's friend. My buddy Wallace had been talking about some cute redhead he'd met earlier, and it hadn't taken much to put two and two together. "You're Noelle's friend, right?"

She nodded once. "She told you about her husband."

"Yeah." My grin faded away. It wasn't a question, but I answered anyway. "She did."

"She's never really let anyone in since he died." She looked me up and down. Despite her small stature and seemingly pixie-like demeanor, I had the feeling she sized me up for weak spots...and found them. Even more unnerving was the fact that I couldn't tell if she liked me, or if she was about to kick my ass. I fought the urge to move the bag I held in front of my dick. "Don't take that for granted, and don't hurt her."

I shifted on my feet. I didn't know what exactly Noelle and I were doing, but I knew one thing. It had an expiration date. She was leaving, and I wasn't. "I won't do that. I don't want to hurt her."

"Good." She smiled. It looked sweet and dangerous. "Then I won't have to hurt you. Have a nice night."

Without another word, she joined a group of women, all of whom were staring at me. She picked up her red wine, saluted me with it, and turned away. I'd been dismissed.

Barge in, make your threats, and boldly walk away.

I liked her style.

Shaking my head, I headed for the elevators. As I waited for them to open for me, I smoothed my hair down and took a deep breath. This was stupid. I was starting something with a woman who made me feel more than any other woman had ever made me feel, and she was only in town for a conference.

Hell, I didn't even know where she lived.

I didn't want to hurt her, not because of her friend's warnings, but because I liked her. I wanted her to be happy. I wanted her to laugh and live and have fun. More than anything, I wanted her to be…well…*her*.

The doors opened, and I stepped inside. Maybe I shouldn't be going to her room, since nothing could ever come of this relationship. She was a romance author, and I was a senator's kid who couldn't do anything without running it by his father's team.

And you could be damn sure they wouldn't approve of Noelle.

But something about her called to me, loud and clear, and I was helpless to ignore it. Like a moth to a flame, I would keep chasing after her as long as I could.

Damn the consequences.

Walking up to her door, I raised my fist and knocked. After a few seconds, the latch slid open, and then she was there. "Hey," she said, smiling at me.

All the tension and doubt and stress within me faded away, all with a smile from her. I didn't know what that meant, and I didn't want to know. All I wanted was her. "Hey, yourself."

She glanced at my hands. "You brought food? And…candles?"

"I didn't have a chance to eat." I glanced down at my hands, feeling like an idiot now. "I was hoping we could have dinner together."

Her smile widened. "You mean, like, a date?"

"Yeah." What had seemed like a good idea now seemed silly. "But if it's too stupid—"

"It's not stupid at all." She opened the door wider. "Come in."

Nodding, I walked inside and glanced around. Both beds were made, and it smelled as delicious as I remembered from last night. I hadn't imagined that. And I obviously hadn't imagined my reaction to her, either. This afternoon in my office had confirmed that much. But it wasn't just the addicting physical reaction that got to me.

It was the feeling that she gave me. Like...like I had found *home*. Which was stupid as hell, because I barely even knew her, and she'd be leaving soon.

Homes didn't leave you.

"You look so serious." She tucked her hair behind her ear and smiled. Her dimples popped out. Clothed in a soft grey skirt, a yellow shirt, and no shoes...she looked fucking delightful. Her large breasts pressed against the tight shirt, and her skirt hugged to perfection those curves that drove me wild. "You okay?"

"Yeah. Sorry." I set the bags down and offered her a sheepish smile. "Just lost in thought, I guess."

She nodded. "I know we've had fun, but please know I expect nothing out of this. We can sit and eat and talk all night long for all I care. We don't have to...do anything."

"Noelle, the last thing on my mind is doubt about *that*."

"I'm sure," she said, glancing down at my dick with a smile. "You're a man, after all. But still. You went through a lot last night. You have to be in so much pain."

She reached out and touched my arm sympathetically. I almost forced a shudder to play along with the whole wounded dude act, but I couldn't pretend with her. Not while she was so real. "But the thing is? I'm not."

"You say that, but—"

"No. I'm really not." I held my hands out, laughing uneasily. "I'm not putting on some machismo act here. I'm being dead serious. I am not upset. She lied. She cheated. It's over." Dropping my hands, I shrugged. "I know I should be upset, but I feel nothing. Nothing at all. Not for her, anyway."

She nodded, swallowing hard. "But you have feelings for your best friend."

"*Had*." I curled my hands into fists. "Years ago. Now she's happily married to my other best friend, and if they ever fell apart, I think I would, too. I think I'd be upset more over that than if anything happened to me."

I watched her pull out the silver candlesticks I'd bought on a whim. She carried them over to the nightstand, setting them down gently.

Reaching into the bag, she pulled out the lighter and lit the candles. The soft glow of the flames washed over her face, and I swallowed hard. It seemed unrealistic and stupid, but something in my gut told me that if we had met under different circumstances, I could feel something for her.

But maybe that's why I had chosen her. Because I knew she'd be leaving, so we could never actually be anything. It was all part of the big picture that said I couldn't allow myself to love anyone or anything, which was pretty fucked up.

"These are pretty." She trailed her fingers over the silver. "They look and feel so real. Like something you'd see in a medieval castle or something."

I swallowed back my reply. They *were* real silver. But something told me she wouldn't be impressed that I'd dropped a few grand to bring a couple of candles to our makeshift date, so I said nothing.

She glanced over her shoulder at me, her profile lit to perfection. "What else is in those bags?"

Snapping back to reality, I forced myself to pay attention. The fact that she was so stunning, so completely enthralling, would never stop amazing me. I could sit with her, watching her smile, laugh, move, for hours and hours.

Oh, shit. Now I sounded like a stalker.

*Great.*

"I brought braised duck, mashed potatoes, and wine." I pulled the containers out of the bag and set them on the bed we'd been in last night. Well, the first bed. "Do you like champagne?"

"Sure." She tucked her hair behind her ear again, looking slightly nervous. "That's quite the feast."

I lifted a shoulder. "I was hungry."

"Obviously."

She perched on the side of the bed, tucking one foot under her butt. The position was unintentionally sexy as hell. Her bright red lips begged for me to kiss them. I had no idea how long I'd be able to spontaneously kiss her, so I did. Bending down, I touched my lips to hers, keeping the kiss light and teasing. She tasted so sweet and sunny that I didn't want to let go, but I wanted to do this right.

We might both know that this was a dalliance, but I wanted to woo her. She deserved romance and kindness. Hell, she deserved it all.

One day, I hoped she got it. Inexplicably, the idea of her with another man didn't sit well. In fact, it bothered me more than Sarah and her ex had. Weird.

Pulling back, I tenderly touched her cheek, marveling over how soft her skin was. It occurred to me I knew nothing about her—and I wanted to know it all. "Hi. I'm Riley Stapleton. I'm a lawyer, and I live here in San Diego."

Her lips curved into a breathtaking smile. "Are we actually doing this?"

"Yep."

She laughed softly. "Hi. I'm Noelle Brandt, but I write dirty but fun romance novels under the name K.M. Reed. Nice to meet you."

"Nice to meet you." I grabbed the bottle of champagne I'd bought. "Tell me. What do you like most about being a writer?"

"I get to work from home in my pajamas, and I have an excuse to drink copious amounts of coffee and booze—because deadlines and edits and reviews drive me to it." She smiled. "What do you like most about being a lawyer?"

"Nothing at all. It's a job I've been told is mostly held by stuffy guys in suits who would never fuck a woman on the first night."

She gasped. "You don't say?"

"I *do*." I popped the cork. It banged into the wall, and we both laughed. Turning back to her, I held the bottle up triumphantly. "Success."

"Hm. Something's wrong." She pursed her lips. Standing, she ruffled my hair again. Then she loosened my tie and patted my chest. "There. Much better."

I grinned. She seemed to prefer me sloppy. It was such a refreshing change. Everyone else demanded I be perfect—and look perfect—at any given time of the day. "How old are you, Noelle?"

"Twenty-six." She took the cup I offered her. "You?"

"Thirty-one." I poured myself a glass and sat beside her. "I grew up in D.C., then went to college here in California."

"D.C., huh?" She sipped her drink. "What do your parents do?"

"My mom is a full supporter of my father's career. My father is, well…" I lifted my drink and mumbled, "He's in law, too. My whole family comes from a long line of…lawyers. And lawmaking."

Her eyes widened. "Really?"

I winced. Maybe I should come clean and tell her he wasn't a businessman, but instead a senator who might be the future vice president, but I didn't want to. She liked me without knowing all that shit, and I liked that about her. For once, I didn't have to wonder if someone only liked me because of my last name.

"Yeah. All the way back to our Founding Fathers."

"Holy shit," she said, her lips curving into a smile. "That's cool."

I nibbled on her throat, and she arched her neck for me. "Not really. Where's the last place you went on vacation?"

Her lashes lowered. "Uh…I don't know. I usually only travel for work, but the last place I went was Houston. You?"

"Hawaii. It's lovely there."

"I—" She swallowed. "I was supposed to honeymoon there."

"But you didn't?" I asked, stiffening at her mention of her ex. For a minute, I'd forgotten she'd already loved and lost. "Why not?"

"He died." She gripped her knees. "So I didn't go."

"Noelle…" I cupped the back of her head gently, my heart breaking for her. "Shit, I'm sorry. So fucking sorry."

She nodded once. "I know. It sucks."

"It really does." I skimmed my finger over her jawline, keeping my touch light. "Are you still…mourning him?"

"I'll always mourn him. I loved him all my life." She licked her lips. "But I've moved on, and I am trying to live my life without him, no matter how much it might hurt. It's what he'd want me to do. So…I'm trying to do that."

I stopped touching her skin, and dropped my hand back in my lap. This conversation might seem too deep for our first "date," but it seemed fitting even so. "How's that working for you?"

"All right. I mean, I'm here with you right now, aren't I?" She cupped my cheek gently. It did weird things to my heart. "You make me feel…I don't know. Alive. Or something. And it feels pretty good."

Something twisted inside me. "You do the same thing to me." Pushing off her, I sat back down and opened the containers of food. "Now, back to that date…"

# chapter ten

## Noelle

I sat back up, my mind spinning like crazy. This man, the one who'd swept me off my feet, was fast becoming more important to me than he should. It hurt to look at him and know our time was running short, because there was no doubt in my mind that eventually Riley would love someone besides his unavailable best friend.

He'd get married and live happily ever after.

While I...

Did what? I had no idea, but I didn't fool myself into thinking this could ever be something that had a shelf life or anything. This was an extended one-night stand.

Nothing more. Nothing less.

He cleared his throat. "So, what do your parents do?"

I flinched. I didn't want to answer this question. My past was my past, and after finding out he'd grown up among a family of lawyers that dated back to our Founding Fathers, he'd never understand *mine*. His parents worked to uphold the law.

Mine had broken it...repeatedly.

So I settled for, "My mom worked in a shop, and my dad was in business."

"Was? Are they both dead?"

They might as well be. I didn't want anything to do with them. Not anymore. Not ever. Besides, they were each serving a life sentence for murdering two shopkeepers in a botched robbery. There was a reason I never went home. Everyone there hated me, with good reason. Everyone except Roger and Emily. Nodding, I said, "Well, yeah. Something like that."

"I'm sorry." He gripped my hand and squeezed. "You've lost so many people."

"It's nothing." I smiled and took the food he offered me. I'd never had duck, but I was willing try anything once. "It's all old news, ya know?"

"Sure." He nodded. "But still, it must suck."

"It does, I guess." Shrugging, I avoided his eyes before I blurted out the truth. Needing to change the subject, I turned the topic back to him. "So, do you like law?"

"Honestly?" He glanced away. "Not really."

I chewed slowly. Turned out duck was delicious. After I swallowed, I asked, "Then why did you go to school for it?"

He shrugged. "It's what was expected of me, so I did it."

I cocked my head. "Do you always do what's expected of you?"

"In the end, yeah. I do."

He seemed almost irritated at this. It made me wonder why he did everything that was expected of him if it made him angry. "Is that why you were going to marry your fiancée? Because it was expected of you?"

He looked a little uncomfortable. "Yeah. Pretty much. They wanted me to marry my best friend, Carrie, but that didn't work out so well."

"Because she fell for someone else, right?"

"Yeah, her husband. He's awesome." He shrugged. "She was in love with him before we met, so I never stood a chance."

"Do you still have feelings for her?" I asked.

"Nah. Not like that." He fidgeted with his fork. "I used to, but not anymore."

I nodded, sensing his desire to move on to another topic. "If you could have been whatever you wanted, what would it be?"

He laughed. "I've never told anyone this, but when I was a kid," he ruffled his hair with his free hand, "I wanted to be a mystery writer. I even wrote a book in college."

"No shit." I grabbed his arm and squeezed. "You should totally do it. What's stopping you from being a writer? Why can't you do it? Don't you want people to read your work?"

He lifted a shoulder, but his eyes were lit up with excitement. "First off? Hell no. No one will ever read that piece of shit. It was awful.

Second off? I will never try to actually publish a book. It's stupid, and not a realistic career."

"You could totally make a career from writing. Lots of people do it. I speak from experience," I said drily.

"Not in my family," he muttered. "In my family, we're sensible and we make the right choices. So I went to law school like they wanted me to."

I shook my head. "Who told you writing was stupid?"

"My parents." He finished his duck. After he swallowed, he said, "But it's fine. I make a good living as a lawyer. I'm financially stable, and I have an excellent firm behind me. And I'm..."

*Empty*, I finished for him silently in my head. And I knew exactly how that felt. He was miserable in his career, and he didn't even know it. I glanced at the expensive champagne bottle. More than likely, it cost more than a month's electricity did at my place. Money could buy lots of things, but it didn't give you what truly mattered in life. Love. Happiness. Fulfillment. He needed that.

"Good." I gestured at the bottle. "Maybe you can buy some happiness with all that cash. I think you'll find it right next to the booze in the store."

He rolled his eyes. "I tried to buy a wife, and look where that got me."

"You —" I swallowed the last of my food and set my container aside. "You have an interesting way of looking at life. You can't *buy* a wife."

"Are you so sure about that? Sarah and I had a business arrangement. She would stay at my side and provide support, and I would keep her well provided for and protect her. Buy her all the nice things she could ever want, and all I asked for in return was that she be mine. No love. No emotions. Business, clear and precise and cold." He picked up our glasses. "If that's not buying a wife, I don't know what is."

"Since you returned her to the store, you should see if they have a return policy." I sipped my wine. "Maybe you can get your money back, minus a re-shelving fee."

He choked on his wine, his face turning red. "Fuck, that was hilarious. Can I keep you? Are you for sale? Name your price."

I fluttered my lashes at him. "Baby, you couldn't afford me."

"Try me." He tipped his wine back and finished it in one gulp, so I did the same. Grinning, he set them both aside and trailed a hand down my arm. Goose bumps followed in his wake, and I shivered. "Tell me more about yourself. Where did you grow up?"

"Connecticut." I bit my lip, refusing to go into more detail than that. No way. No how. "But I'm in New York now, in the city."

Easier to blend in with the crowds there, and try to forget my old life. Back home, everyone hated my family. We'd lived in a small town, and my parents had murdered beloved people there.

Riley looked at me and frowned. "New York City? That's so far away."

"Yeah. It is."

He stared at me, and I didn't break eye contact. "Shit."

My heart picked up speed. The way he was looking at me, with possessiveness and sadness, interlaced together, sent warmth rushing through my veins.

He ruffled his hair. "This is stupid. I figured you probably didn't live here, and yet…"

"I know." I bit down on my lower lip. "I feel the same way."

"How much longer do we have together?"

I swallowed. "Three more days."

"Noelle…" He dropped his hand in his lap. "That's not enough time with you, damn it. I wanted more."

"I know. Me too."

He stared into my eyes, then his gaze drifted down to my mouth. With a strangled groan, he closed the distance between us. The second he touched his mouth to mine, I knew we had something special between us. Something we could take with us, once this was over, and remember forever. If I wished it could last longer than a few days, then oh well. Life was life.

And we weren't meant to be.

His mouth moved over mine, and I opened mine with a sigh. As he kissed me, he crawled on top of me, urging me to lie down. I followed his lead. As soon as my back hit the mattress, his hands were everywhere. They skimmed over my hips, down my thighs, and over the flat of my stomach.

Breaking the kiss off, he looked down at me with heated eyes. "You're so gorgeous, Noelle. Inside and out, you are perfection."

I'd never get sick of hearing him say that. "So are you."

"Bull. I'm not pretty." He smirked and lowered his voice to a baritone. "I'm manly and handsome."

Laughing, I nodded. "Yeah. You are." I touched the dimple in his chin. I loved that dimple. "And for now, you're all mine. That has to be enough."

He slid his hand up my skirt. "And you're mine." His fingers touched the skin right under my panty line, and he skimmed his fingers over me. "Now take these all off for me."

I licked my dry lips. "You want a strip tease?"

"Hell yeah I do." He rolled over on his side on the bed, tugging his tie looser, and then pulling it over his head. When I didn't get up, he raised a cocky brow. He motioned me with his fingers. "If you're offering, I'm accepting. It's all I could think about all afternoon."

Standing up, I smiled seductively. "Then far be it for me not to provide."

Grabbing the hem of my shirt, I pulled it over my head slowly, wiggling my hips as I did so. After I pulled it over my head, I tossed it at him. "Now you."

He tossed my shirt aside. Sitting up straight, he undid the buttons. Once it lay open, he shot me the dirtiest look I've ever seen on a man's face. One that sent a shaft of desire piercing through me and made my knees go weak. He shrugged the shirt off, his muscles flexing as he moved. "Next item of clothing."

Locking gazes with him, I wiggled out of my skirt. His deep indrawn breath sent shivers down my spine. Already, I was wet and wanting. And we weren't even naked yet. Holding the skirt with my pinky, I let it hit the floor. I raised a brow at him.

He raked his gaze down my body, skimming over my matching red panty and bra set, and stood. His hands trembled as he undid his belt, then his pants. He pulled the belt out of the loops and set it on the bed, then let his pants hit the floor. He had on a pair of black boxer briefs, and they hugged his erection with picture-perfect clarity. He was as huge as I remembered him being. "Riley…"

He took a step toward me, every motion he made claiming his dominance over me. And I loved it. "Take the bra off."

Lifting my chin, I steadied my nerves and undid the clasp, letting it fall down my arms and hit the floor with my skirt. Without him asking, I gripped my panties and tugged them down. I stood in front of him, naked and quivering with so much desire it hurt. I needed him. Needed his touch. So freaking badly.

I'd never felt this way about a guy, and part of me had been so sure that intense attraction had been driven by my drunkenness last night. But I hadn't been drunk in his office, and I wasn't drunk now. He just drove me crazy, pushing me further and further until I exploded.

"Jesus." He walked to me, trailing a finger over my ribcage. Such a simple touch, but the things it did to my body were anything but simple. "Look at you. So fair. So pretty. And the best part?" He swept my hair to the side, his fingers gliding over my skin as he did so. "You're as pretty on the inside as you are on the outside."

I swallowed hard. "If you say so."

"Who else finds a drunk stranger and somehow makes him feel like he's flown off this earth and into some sort of heaven with simply a smile?" He kissed my shoulder, behind my neck. "Who else has the power to bring me to my knees if she wanted, but doesn't exert it?"

I laughed uneasily. "I wouldn't mind it if you went on your knees right around now."

He chuckled huskily, the sound made of pure, raw sex. Without a word, he dropped to his knees in front of me. At some point, he'd removed his boxers, and he was naked. Gloriously, amazingly *naked*. Tipping his head back, he smirked. "Ask, and you shall receive..."

I threaded my hands in his hair and swallowed a moan. "Oh my God, yes."

Leaning in, he flicked his tongue over my sensitive clit, moaning when he tasted me. Without warning, he urged my legs apart, helping me keep my balance. Then he spread me with two fingers, and closed his mouth over me. I cried out, digging my nails into his scalp, and squeezed my eyes shut.

He moved his tongue over me, tantalizing and teasing me with each stroke. Each movement drove me higher and higher, and I knew it wouldn't be long before I exploded.

When he reached up and cupped my breasts with his hands, squeezing the nipples tight, I almost collapsed. Somehow I managed to keep my shit together, though. But then, I couldn't. The pleasure he'd awoken burst me into pieces, and I was letting out shuddered breaths and saying words I didn't even understand.

He pushed me back on the bed, and then he was on me, kissing me and touching me, and urging the fire on even more. I closed my legs around his waist, and he was there, his erection pressed against my core. So close, but not close enough.

He cupped my face and kissed me, even his kiss claiming dominance over me. It felt as if he was staking a claim, and I wished he was. I wanted to be his in every way.

It was a startling thought.

Skimming my hands down his body, I closed my fingers around his huge erection. He moaned into my mouth, pumping into my hand. A drip of semen escaped, and I rubbed it in with my thumb. "Fuck," he gasped, dropping his forehead on mine. "I wanted to go slow, but I need you, Noelle. I need you so fucking bad."

I nodded frantically, the urgency still a very real thing. "Yes. Please, *now*."

He pushed back and grabbed a condom out of the bag on the other bed, his eyes locked on me the whole time. I licked my lips and watched as he rolled it on. "Next time, I'm securing your wrists with my belt and I'm going to lick you all over. Understood?"

My stomach hollowed out. "Anything you want is yours. Just take me now."

"Yes, ma'am."

Grinning, he lowered his body over mine, sliding his hands under my butt to pull me up. As soon as he had me where he wanted me, he thrust into me. He was huge, and he stretched me in ways I'd never been stretched. He only thrust partially inside me, pausing and breathing heavily. After a few breaths, he pulled out and thrust again, still not entering me all the way.

Sweat broke out on his forehead. "Jesus, Noelle."

"More." I cried out, gripping the sheets under me and arching my back. "Give me more."

He didn't pause or hesitate. He pulled out and thrust back in, hitting the spot that I had begun to doubt existed. He'd given me more, but still not all of him. "You feel so good."

"*Riley.*"

"I'm here, babe, I'm here." He flexed his fingers on my skin, squared his jaw, and locked gazes with me. "I'm not going anywhere."

I bit down on my lip so hard, I tasted blood. The man was some kind of orgasm wizard or something. Tap your fingers together three times, and *bam*. There it was.

My hands fisted the sheets, and I locked my feet together behind his back. He pulled almost all the way out, then slammed back into me. His whole body was rock hard, and I could tell he was still holding himself back from me.

I dug my nails into his back. "More. Give me all you have."

"I don't want to…" He rolled his hips into me, sweat on his forehead. "Hurt you."

"You won't." I cupped his cheeks, staring into those eyes I'd never forget. "Take me, Riley. All of me."

Something inside of him seemed to break. He collapsed on top of me, merging his mouth with mine, and thrust into me fully. I'd thought he'd been big earlier? I'd been wrong. Having all of him buried inside me, stretching me, was more than I'd ever dreamed of. Crying out, I dug my nails into his back and lifted my hips. "*More.*"

He kissed me even harder, his tongue slashing against mine as he moved his hips faster and deeper and harder. I clung to him, my hand roaming everywhere I could touch, and then before I knew it, I was coming again. He kept kissing me, touching me, and thrust into me even harder.

I cried out, unable to believe he was bringing me back up that crest again. With a growl, he flipped me over effortlessly in his arms, never fully withdrawing. When I was on all fours, he gripped my hips and entered me from behind, even deeper than before.

I buried my face in my pillow and screamed obscenities as the desire rose higher and higher and then the pleasure exploded again.

This time, he was right there with me, his body going stiff behind me as he came, too.

With a shuddering sigh, he collapsed on the bed, pulling me with him. "Noelle," he breathed, kissing my temple from behind. "My sweet, sweet Noelle."

Grinning, I buried my face into the pillow again. "I don't know how sweet I was just now. Naughty, maybe…"

"Sweet." He kissed my head this time. "Always sweet."

We both fell silent, simply laying in each other's arms and enjoying the moment. After a few minutes, he lazily traced a pattern on my bare thigh. "Why is there a ballgown and mask hanging on your bathroom door?"

I chuckled. "We have a masquerade party tomorrow night. I'm dressing up for it."

"Oh. That sounds fun."

I smiled and snuggled closer. "It should be. I've always liked balls, even as a teenager."

Choking on a laugh, he asked, "Did you seriously just say that to me?"

"Oh, come on," I said smacking him on the chest. The smile, however, was inescapable. "You know what I meant."

"I did," he said, still laughing. After he stopped, he inhaled deeply and smoothed his fingers over my hair. Smiling, I closed my eyes and relaxed, slowly drifting off until he asked, "What was he like?"

"Who?" I asked sleepily, forcing my eyes open. His soft touch had been lulling me to sleep. "What was who like?"

"Your husband." He reached out and picked up my hand, his thumb tracing the diamond band I'd never taken off. To take it off had seemed wrong. But now, lying in bed with Riley, it felt almost wrong to still be wearing it. I tucked my hand under the pillow, uncomfortable with looking at it right now. "Was he a good man?"

"He was." I curled my hand into a fist under my pillow. "One of the best I've ever known. We fell in love in middle school, and we were together up until the day he died. Even after everything I'd gone through…all the shit I dealt with…he never left me. Never doubted me. Never made me feel like less than what I was."

Riley swallowed hard. I couldn't see it, but I could feel it since he rested his chin on my head. "You loved him."

"I loved — love — him a lot."

"Would you ever love anyone else?" He tugged on a piece of my hair, staring at it as if it contained all the answers to his unasked questions. "Think you'd ever love like that again?"

"I don't know," I answered honestly. "Loving someone like that…

it opens you up to a lot of pain. They could leave you. Hurt you. Die. I don't know if I'd want to do that all over again. I never thought I would have survived it, after he left me..."

"What happened?" He smoothed my hair off my face, his touch gentle and barely there. "How did he die?"

I closed my eyes, remembering every terrible detail of that night. "We got married a year and a half ago. Our wedding was magical and perfect. The thing was, I didn't have a chance to eat. By the time we got to our hotel room, my stomach was so empty it was eating itself alive. I was dizzy and cranky and I needed food."

He nodded behind me. "I've heard that's a common thing for brides."

"Yeah. Well..." I opened my eyes, starting at the wall. The empty ache that was inside me throbbed, and I knew it would never fully go away. "He wanted to feed me, even though I was being a royal bitch to him because my sugar was so low. After kissing me on the head, he went to his car, got in, and I never saw him again. He was hit by a drunk driver on his way to get me some dinner."

"Noelle...*no.*"

I closed my eyes. "He died because I was too stupid to eat at my own wedding. If I'd just had a bite of chicken or a forkful of cake..."

"Look at me." I did. He rolled me over on my back, his sympathetic green eyes filled with so much sadness. "Don't do that to yourself. Don't make this into something you did. You couldn't have known that someone would sit behind a wheel, drunk off his ass, and take that happiness away from you."

I shook my head. "I didn't, but still. It was my fault. I should have eaten."

"No." He kissed my nose, his hands still framing my face. "He would never want you to think like that, I bet." He kissed my lips gently. "I didn't know him, but if you loved him so much, he must've been an amazing guy."

"He was."

"Well then, he'd want you to know that he did what he did because he loved you. His passing is horrible and tragic and sad, but it's *not your fault.*"

I'd heard that from plenty of people, in plenty of ways. But for some reason, coming from Riley, it made perfect sense. I almost believed him. For the sake of keeping the night happy, I nodded and forced a smile. "You're right."

He eyed me skeptically. "And you're lying. You don't believe me."

"Riley..."

"It's okay. One day you will." He smiled down at me. "One day you'll believe me. Even if I'm not there, you'll be sitting there in your living room, doing a crossword puzzle, and you'll look up, your eyes lighting up. With a soft smile, you'll say, 'He was right. Riley was right.'"

I had a feeling he believed it, but I didn't. That guilt would be something I'd carry around with me forever. My parents had killed two people, and I'd killed one. I was just as guilty as they were. It must run in my family. But I didn't want to argue. "You should totally write another book. That was quite the scene you just described."

A grin broke out on his face. "Thanks."

"Anytime." The moment between us was so intense I had to look away. Glancing down at his arm, I traced a thin scar on his forearm. "What's this from?"

"An abduction gone wrong."

"*What?*" I looked at it again. "Seriously?"

"Yeah. I was with Carrie, and they took us by surprise. She'd just gotten in a fight with Finn, and then he was gone, and she was panicking, and then they had us." He shrugged his shoulders, still holding his weight with his elbows. "I talked back and got that scar for my efforts."

"You're only a lawyer's son. Why the abduction?"

"I guess we looked like a quick payday?" He averted his face, his body tense against mine. "I don't know. But we're fine, obviously."

I swallowed hard. "Your life is so different from mine."

"What?" He raised a brow. "You've never been abducted in an attempt for ransom? Doesn't that happen to everyone at some point or another in their lives?"

I snorted. "Not me. No one would pay a ransom for me, so it would be a waste of the kidnappers' time. They'd end up offing me and dumping me in the Hudson, which is so gross."

He sobered. "I would pay for you."

"Ha!"

"It's true." He looked down into my eyes, his looking way too honest and open for my own good. "You're worth more than a million dollars, or a king's ransom in jewels. Your value is immeasurable. Don't ever doubt it."

I shook my head. "You barely even know me."

"I know enough to know I would pay." He twisted his lips. "To be fair, I'd pay for a friend, too, but I like to think we're more than friends. I like to think we're something special."

Smiling, I resisted the urge to press a hand to my melting heart. "Oh, we are. And you're the one who's sweet. Not me."

"No way." He shook his head. "You take that award, hands down.

Thank you for seeing something good in me last night, and for letting me in your room. And thank you for coming to my office to set me straight. I'm very happy to have met you, Noelle Brandt. Whatever comes of this, I'm happy to have met you."

I forced a smile. "That sounds an awful lot like a goodbye."

"Not yet." He hesitated. "But as much as I hate to think of it, our time will be over soon. I don't want to forget to tell you these things, so I'll say them when they pop in my head. That way I don't miss a thing."

Tears filled my eyes. Men like him weren't supposed to be real. He was too sweet to be real. "It's kind of sad, isn't it?"

"It is." He lay back down and pulled me into his arms, letting out a long sigh. "New York, huh?"

My heart picked up speed. "Yep."

"Do you live in the city?"

I shook my head. "In Queens."

"I've been to the city a few times, but I never went out to Queens."

"Really?" I said, completely unsurprised. My tiny apartment in a shady part of town was a far cry from the penthouse suites he probably stayed in.

But, hey, it was mine.

Roger and I had been planning on staying in that apartment until we started a family, but then he'd died. And I'd stayed. We hadn't been there the night he'd died. We'd been in a hotel near the airport. He'd never come back.

But I had.

Riley dropped his head on mine. "Are you sure you're not for sale?"

I snorted. "Careful, I might think you're serious."

"What tells you I'm not?" he asked, his voice teasing.

If he kept saying things like that, it was going to be even harder to walk away than I'd ever imagined. Already, I knew it was going to be one of the most difficult things I'd ever have to do. But this was a short-term thing. A fun fling.

Even if I wished it *could* be more...

# chapter eleven

## Riley

The next morning, I woke up slowly. Through my fog-drenched sleep, I felt her hand skimming over my body. At first, I thought I was dreaming, but then she closed her mouth over my dick, and I jerked awake. And being awake turned out to be so much more fucking excellent than it being a dream.

She knelt between my legs, her beautiful bare ass sticking up in the air, and watched me as she lowered those red lips over me again, taking more of me in than I'd have thought possible. My eyes rolled back in my head, and I buried my hands in her soft, curly hair.

"Noelle."

Cupping my balls with her hand, she took more of me in, sucking hard and rolling her tongue over the head of my dick at the same time. I groaned and arched my hips experimentally, not wanting to give her too much. She moaned and took more of me in, her sexy mouth driving me to heights I'd never been before.

This woman almost had my heart in her hands, not my balls, and she didn't even know it. Okay, that was way too metaphorical for me, but she definitely had gotten closer to my heart than I'd ever thought someone could.

Every moment I spent with her, she dug her claws in deeper.

It wasn't just the sex, or the attraction. It was *every*thing. It was all of her. She made me laugh and feel good. I wanted to keep her forever and ever and ever.

"Marry me," I whispered.

As soon as the words were out of my mouth, I froze. Had I really—?

She choked on my cock, her arms flailing as she sucked in a deep breath. Cringing, I helped her pull back, my cheeks hot. They were probably redder than her panties on the floor. She settled back on her haunches, her eyes wide, and swiped a hand over her mouth before bursting into laughter. "You can't say something like that when I'm doing *that*. I mean, I know you're not serious, but *still*."

"Uh…" I froze. She didn't think I was serious. I could laugh it off like she had. Pretend I hadn't meant it, even though I kind of did. "Who says I didn't mean it?"

Her laughter died. "You didn't. You couldn't."

I cocked a brow at her but didn't say a word. Hell, even I wasn't sure if I was serious. Not yet.

"Did you just actually propose to me, for real, while your cock was in my mouth?" she asked.

I laughed uneasily. What the hell was I supposed to say after that? I could claim it was a mistake. A moment I'd been lost in the heat of her mouth fucking me. But in reality, it wasn't just a moment of madness. At least I didn't think it was.

She stared at me, her eyes even wider and her hand pressed to her mouth. The same mouth that had been driving me insane seconds earlier. "Riley…"

"Shh." I rolled her under me, nibbling on her neck once she bounced off the mattress. "Don't answer yet."

She opened her mouth to talk, but I kissed her before she could answer me. Before she could do the smart thing and say *hell no*. When my tongue dipped into her mouth, I swallowed her long moan. Damn, I loved those moans. My hand slipped between her legs, and she broke off the kiss with a gasp.

"Riley, I—"

I dropped my forehead on hers. "Don't say it. Don't say no. Don't say anything at all."

She lifted her arms, hesitated, but then kissed me again, her soft lips yielding to mine exquisitely. Groaning, I kissed her back, taking control again. As soon as she relaxed in my arms, my phone rang. I ignored it, but as soon as it stopped it started again. I didn't answer it.

When it rang a third time, she broke the kiss off. "Riley." She tapped my arm. "You better answer that."

Cursing under my breath, I answered without looking at the caller ID, my body still on top of hers, the irritation clear and crisp in my

70

Jen McLaughlin

---

voice. "Hello?"

"It's me. Sarah. You're not in the office," Sarah said, her voice soft.

I stiffened, my gaze flying to Noelle, who went completely still underneath me. Had she heard the feminine voice? I had no clue. Just like I had no clue why Sarah was calling me after all she'd done to me. "And you know that because…?"

"I came here. I…I wanted to talk to you."

Noelle arched a brow, and I offered her a small, reassuring smile before replying. "Why would you need to talk to me?"

"It's just…" Sarah sobbed, her voice cracking. "He left me again."

Closing my eyes, I rolled off Noelle and sat up. When I looked at her again, she pulled the covers up to her chin, her bright hazel eyes locked on me.

"Everything okay?" she whispered.

Nodding once, I turned my attention back to my ex. "I'm sorry. But I fail to see how this affects me."

Noelle looked away, her cheeks red.

"I made a mistake. I'm so sorry, Riley. I think it was just pre-wedding jitters."

I laughed. "Pre-wedding jitters? Seriously?"

"Riley…"

"No. I'm not doing this." I stood up, completely naked and not giving a damn. Noelle slipped a robe on, watching me the whole time. I paced back and forth, my hand locked behind my neck. "It's over, Sarah. *Over.*"

She sobbed. "I'm sorry I did this to us. I did love you, you know."

"No, you didn't." Something inside me twisted. "You told me that."

"I was scared," she cried. "Please come into the office and talk to me. We can—"

"No. We have nothing to discuss. Not anymore. Be gone before I get there," I warned. "We're over."

Hanging up, I tossed my phone on the bed and turned to Noelle. She watched me, her eyes cautious and her cheeks flushed. She looked so pretty standing there, wearing nothing more than a pink robe. "So… that was her? The ex?"

"Yeah." I lifted a shoulder. "It doesn't matter though."

"Oh, but it does." She reached me and stopped directly in front of me. "She wants you back."

"She does," I admitted. I grabbed a curl of hers and wrapped it around my finger. She let me. "But I don't give a damn what she wants. Not anymore."

"But you always do what's expected of you. That's what you said."

Raising a brow, I tugged on the curl. She came a step closer, but she stopped there. "And?"

"Will it be expected for you to forgive her? To marry her?"

Again, I lifted a shoulder. "I don't think so. My mom was pretty pissed."

"Your *mom*?"

"Yeah." I tugged again. She didn't move. "Why do you look so upset?"

"Because you're going to get back together with her, and that makes me sad. You deserve more than what she can give you." She rested her hands on my chest. My phone buzzed at the same time. "She doesn't deserve a guy like you."

My heartbeat increased at her touch. In fact, it was like my whole body came to life. Every. Single. Part. It was like every piece of me wanted her to stay nearby, touching me. I had no idea what the fuck that meant, but I think it was a good thing.

I needed to talk to someone who knew what this feeling was.

"She doesn't?"

She shook her head slowly, her hazel eyes locked on mine. My phone buzzed twice in a row. "No. Not at all."

"That's good," I said, grabbing her hips and urging her closer. "Because I don't want to marry her anymore."

I wisely refrained from reminding her I'd asked her to marry me moments before...while my dick was in her mouth. I got the distinct impression she didn't want to talk about that. Or say yes. I didn't know how I felt about that yet.

"Good." Raising up on tiptoe, she pressed her mouth to mine. "Remember that you deserve better. You deserve love and happiness. *Real* love. Promise me?"

"Sure, whatever you say." My phone buzzed again, and I tightened my grip on her hips. I didn't want to let go...well, ever. "Damn it."

"Now go to work. I have a feeling you're late, and I have a workshop to go to in thirty minutes anyway." She stepped back, ducking her head and hiding her eyes from me. "And someone's apparently waiting for you."

"I told her to leave."

"She won't," Noelle said, her mouth pressed in a tight line. "She'll be there, with big old fat tears in her eyes."

I cocked my head. "Are you jealous of her?"

"What? N-No."

"Damn." I picked up my bag and headed into the bathroom. "I'd been hoping you cared enough to be jealous."

She balled her hands into fists but didn't reply. Just watched as I went into the bathroom and shut the door behind me. The whole time I showered, my mind was on that proposal. I mean, I'd never really been much of a romantic, so to speak, but even I knew that what I'd done was a big no-no.

Although, in a way, it just might be the most romantic thing I'd ever done. I was big on thinking things through. On weighing pros and cons, and never acting on impulse. I didn't do something spur of the moment, and I never acted on emotion and emotions alone. But with her, that's pretty much all I'd done so far.

From the moment I'd laid eyes on her, my brain had ceased functioning. Instead, I'd relied on my gut, my wants, my desires, and my...fuck it. Yeah, my *heart*.

That didn't mean I was going to go so far as to say I loved her. I wasn't that far gone. But I knew one thing. The guy she made me? The one I was with her?

I kind of liked him.

And I think she liked him, too.

Probably not enough to actually marry me or anything, but still. She liked me for me. After I'd wrapped a towel around my waist, I came out of the bathroom talking. "I know that my words were crazy, but—"

I broke off because there was no point in continuing. I was alone in the hotel room. On the untouched bed, there was a note.

> Riley,
> I've had a nice time, but under the circumstances, I think it's best if it ends here. I'll be leaving soon, and really, it's best if we take the magical nights we had and hold them close to our hearts. Good luck with your life, and please remember...you deserve more than an arranged marriage. You deserve love. And you are capable of love. I know it, and deep down, so do you.
> Noelle

I closed my fist on the note, my heart wrenching painfully. If I deserved better, as she said, then I deserved her. And if I deserved better, I should have gotten more than a note as a goodbye. Apparently, she'd had enough of me and my emotional, thoughtless actions. If she truly thought I deserved better...

Then why did she leave me?

My phone rang again. I glanced at it, stupidly hoping it was her. It wasn't. It was my mother. Bending down, I picked it up. "Hello?"

"Riley, it's me. Your mother."

I rolled my eyes. "Yes, I know."

"Who is this woman you've been seen with? This Noelle Brandt woman?"

I froze. "How did you—?"

"It doesn't matter."

"Yes, it does. Who told you? Hell, *I* didn't even tell anyone."

"Language, Riley." She sighed. "Reginald saw you last night. He was at the hotel for a business dinner, and he said he saw you talking to some short-haired romance writer. And you went up to her room. I did some digging around, and I figured out who she was."

They hadn't even seen Noelle. She had no idea what was going on, and yet she still felt the need to shove her nose into things. "Wow. You guys seriously need a life if me talking to some girl in a hotel is news in your circle."

"Enough sass, Riley. Please tell me she's a dalliance and nothing more. A one-night stand to get back at Sarah, or to sow some wild oats. You know you can't marry a romance writer, of all things."

I'd wanted her to be more, but that obviously wasn't going to happen. I glanced down at the note again, my chest tight. Though I should tell my mother it was none of her business, because it wasn't, I didn't. It was over, so there was nothing to defend anymore. "It's nothing. We're nothing."

It wasn't a lie. Not really. Noelle had just proved to me that we were nothing by leaving me with a fucking *note*. If she could do that?

We'd never been anything at all.

# chapter twelve

## Noelle

I walked down the hallway, my breathing coming calm and yet unsteady. I'd left the room and gone to breakfast alone, but it hadn't helped me relax. Not after Riley had proposed to me while I'd been giving him a blowjob, and then basically said he'd meant it. That was crazy. Insane.

But I hadn't been able to stop thinking about it ever since, because in a way I'd almost wanted to say yes, which was even more insane than him asking me in the first place. But I'd done things the slow and steady way.

I'd taken my time, fallen in love slowly and surely, and been engaged for three years before actually saying I do. And then it had all been snatched out of my hands.

If that had shown me anything, it was that life was unpredictable and cruel. If you were lucky enough to find happiness, any happiness, maybe you should grab it with both hands, and never let go. Maybe you should be crazy and say yes.

Or, maybe you should listen to the voice of reason in the back of your head that said you shouldn't marry a guy you just met...if he'd even really meant that proposal.

Emily came up to me, her face lit up with excitement. "Hey! Guess what? I just got an agent!"

All thoughts of Riley and any crazy proposals faded away. "What? Oh my God! Congratulations! Who?"

"Tiffany Crown." Emily jumped up and down, looking happier than I'd seen her in a long, long time. A year and a half, to be exact. "From After Thoughts Agency."

"Wow. She's great!" I hugged her close. "I knew you'd get an offer, but this is fabulous. We have to celebrate."

"It's only eleven." Emily looked at her phone. "But it's five o'clock somewhere. Let's go get a mimosa or something."

"Absolutely," I said, grinning so widely it hurt. "Which book is she going to shop around first?"

Emily started for the hotel bar. "The motorcycle hero."

"Hot," I said, nodding. "Wow, look at that. My little Emily, all official and stuff."

Her cheeks turned red. "I took that pinky promise seriously. It doesn't just apply to men and sex. It applies to everything. And I got a freaking *agent*."

We fist-bumped like we'd been doing since elementary school. "On fire, baby."

"I know," Emily agreed, shimmying onto a bar stool and propping her chin in her hands. "I can't believe it actually happened. I actually have an agent."

I sat beside her. "Did you tell her you'd think about it, or did you say yes?"

"Oh, I said yes. She's the agent I wanted, you know? All her clients have good sales, and they all spoke very highly of her."

Nodding, I smiled at the bartender. "Two mimosas, please. And charge them to my room, three-oh-five."

"We should have roomed together," Emily said, pulling her phone out. "Remind me why we didn't?"

"Because Rose was going to room with me, but then she backed out." I shrugged. "And since I haven't been in that room alone…"

"It's probably better I didn't."

"Yep." I forced a smile. Thinking about Riley reminded me I'd ended it with him, but I wasn't going to bring it up. It was time to celebrate, not think about him and whether or not I should have told him we were over in a note. "Pretty much."

"Ugh, I want to tweet this, but I can't."

"Nope." I snatched her phone out of her hand. "Not yet. Not till you sign the papers."

Emily smiled. "Remember when you got your agent?"

"Of course. It's not something you forget," I said, smiling too.

"Roger made me my favorite dinner, and he said we wouldn't be living in that small apartment for much longer because I'd be a New York Times bestselling author. He never got to see it happen, but he was right."

"Yeah, he was." Emily's smile slipped a little bit. "And we went out drinking at that bar under your place. I stumbled home three blocks, drunk off my ass, and knocked on my neighbor's door because I couldn't get the key in my lock."

I choked on a laugh. "You didn't!"

"I did." Emily laughed again. "He helped me open my door, and then helped me open something else."

I facepalmed. "Oh. My. God."

"What?" She wriggled her brows. "A girl's gotta get some every once in a while."

"Well, duh."

"But, anyway. Back to business talk." Our mimosas came, and we both grabbed one. "To new beginnings and exciting adventures?"

I swallowed hard. "Amen."

We sipped our drinks, and I glanced around the bar. I saw a group of readers watching us, whispering amongst themselves. I offered them a smile and turned back to Emily. "What else do you have planned for today, besides world domination?"

"I'm going to that BDSM panel in an hour. Want to go with me?"

I nodded. "Yeah. Sure."

Anything to get my mind off Riley. Had he actually meant that proposal? He couldn't have. Could he? Of course not. But...

"You okay?" Emily asked me.

"Yeah, of course."

I stared at the TV. It was some crime drama show where the cops always caught the bad guys within the hour. I couldn't watch those shows because they reminded me of my parents. My old life. And I didn't like thinking of that.

"Excuse me?" Emily asked. "Can we change the channel?"

The bartender picked up the remote. "Any preferences?"

"Anything but this," Emily said, her eyes on me. "You still think about them sometimes?"

"How could I not? They're my parents. And they're awful and wrong and in jail. I try to ignore them and what they did. But it isn't possible." I ran my finger over the champagne flute. "They're always there."

Emily cocked her head. "What do you mean?"

"It means they're in my past, and I try not to remember them at all, really. But no matter how hard I try to pretend it never happened, they always come to the surface." I downed the rest of my drink. "At one point or another, the truth always comes out."

"Maybe the truth isn't so bad." She finished her drink, too. The bartender had put on a comedy, and she smiled at something one of the characters said. "As much as you've always thought their behavior reflected yours, it doesn't. You're not them."

"Tell that to the people of Connecticut."

"Screw them." She scrunched her nose up. "There's a reason the three of us moved to New York, and it wasn't just because of our writing and Roger's career as an advertising exec."

I smiled. "Fresh starts."

"Fresh faces." Emily smiled back. "And we did it. We started over."

"And now here we are. In a hotel bar. Celebrating."

She hopped off the stool. "Indeed. But now? We have to go get in line for that BDSM panel. I hear it's going to be packed."

"Yay," I said unenthusiastically. "Crowds. My favorite thing."

Emily laughed at me. "You knew there would be crowds. I mean, it's a conference. What did you expect?"

"Exactly this," I muttered. "But we all know how important networking is to this world."

"Indeed. So suck it up, Buttercup. We have a panel to go to."

And a man to try to forget...

Because I'd told him we were done, even though I didn't feel done.

## Riley

I slammed into my office more than a half hour late, but that hadn't stopped Sarah from waiting for me. She sat in front of my desk, perched primly on the edge of the chair. The second I opened the door, she stood, smoothing her pale pink skirt over her legs.

Closing the door behind me, I sighed and walked to my chair. "I'm really not in the mood right now," I snapped.

She flinched, and I almost felt bad. It wasn't her fault I was ready to strangle someone. No, that rested solely on my shoulders. And Noelle's.

But really, *why* had I thought proposing to her like that had been a good idea? I hadn't thought about it at all, that's why. That's what happened to me when I tried being impulsive for once in my life. I fucked it all up.

Sarah fidgeted. "I'm sorry."

I dragged a hand through my hair and forced a calm breath. "I just had a really bad morning is all. But I told you to leave. You should listen to me."

"I wanted to wait for you."

Yeah. Noelle had said as much.

I set my briefcase on the desk a little too hard, my heart twisting at the thought of Noelle. I still couldn't believe she'd dismissed me like that. As if I hadn't mattered to her. Considering the fact that I'd fucking proposed to her, I'd thought that maybe, just maybe, she'd cared about me a tiny bit, too.

I'd been wrong.

Slumping into my chair, I blew out a breath. "Look, Sarah. I don't know what you think you're going to accomplish here, but I'm not interested."

She bit her lip. "I know I hurt you, but I wasn't thinking clearly. I thought…I thought he loved me, and it felt real. I got caught up in the excitement of it all and ignored all the warning signs. You know?"

"I do. I get it." I sighed and pinched the bridge of my nose. Our engagement photo was still on my desk. I needed to get rid of it. "What happened with your ex?"

"We saw each other in the store a few weeks ago, and—"

I held up a hand and frowned at her. "That's not what I meant.

I don't want to know why you fell for him again, because it doesn't matter. You did. I meant why are you here with me instead of him?"

"I'm so sorry, Riley—"

"Don't. I'm not hurt or upset. I'm really not." I dropped my hand to the desk. "Which is why we don't work. Why we can't be together."

She twisted her engagement ring on her finger. She'd put it back on. "Or it's why we make perfect sense. We won't hurt each other. It's safe."

Safe. Such a tame word, one I'd once used to try to make her see why we fit together so perfectly. And she was right. A marriage with her would be perfectly safe. She'd never rip my heart out by writing a goodbye letter to me, and leaving me alone in a hotel room. I shouldn't have proposed to Noelle when she'd been going down on me...

But I had. And she'd run.

That hurt because I liked her so damn much. Yes, it had been a spontaneous proposal, and I hadn't thought it through, but it just might have been my best idea ever.

She made me want to live, have fun, and be free.

Not be a *Stapleton*.

Sarah must have taken my silence for something akin to agreement, because she came around the back of the desk and stopped right next to me. She rested a hand on my shoulder. It made me feel...nothing. Nothing at all.

"Just think about it. I know I made a stupid mistake, but I won't do it again. I learned my lesson, and I'd rather be with you." Hesitantly, she bent down and kissed my forehead. I winced. "We make a good team, you and I."

I tipped my head back. She was only an inch or so away, but I wasn't threatened by the close proximity. "I used to think you were right, but you see...I met someone. Someone who made my heart race and made me want to do crazy things, just because."

Her hand tightened on my shoulder and she straightened. "You met someone?"

"I did."

"Is she...are you...*with* her?"

That was a question I couldn't really answer. Noelle had told me she was done, but I didn't feel done. Not a single part of me felt done. I glowered at the photo of Sarah and me. We were both smiling and holding on to each other as if we actually cared. Things had been so much easier then, but even so, I wouldn't go back.

I'd seen what emotions—*real* emotions—could do, and I wanted that with Noelle. I had to go back to the hotel, find her, and show her we weren't done. If I was this upset, surely she had to be, too. Right?

This couldn't all be one-sided. Not something this strong and insistent. She might be ready to give up because I'd freaked her out with my unromantic proposal, but we could fix this. We could fix us. I just had to go find her.

And that proposal, while ill timed, had been true. Real. I wanted to do it. I wanted to be impulsive and romantic and do something without thinking it through.

I wanted to *marry* her.

"I'm sorry, but yes. We are." Standing, I offered Sarah a small smile. "And I have to go find her. I have to tell her something."

She wrapped her arms around herself. "I hope she knows how lucky she is."

"I don't know that she is, really," I admitted. "But I do hope you and I can be friends. I don't want to marry you, but I don't hate you."

She forced a smile. "I'd like that."

"Good." I squeezed her hand as I passed. "I have to go, I'm sorry."

"I'll tell your secretary you had an emergency." She nodded toward the door. "Go. Go get her. And I hope you find happiness."

Ah, but I had. I'd found it in Noelle.

I just had to ensure she felt it, too.

# chapter thirteen

## Noelle

An hour later, I fidgeted in my seat at the back of the crowded room, my mind a million miles from the current topic of conversation. My mind, of course, was still firmly locked on Riley, and his proposal.

When he'd asked me to marry him while I had been going down on him, I'd been so sure he meant it in a "don't stop what you're doing" type of way, but then he'd acted as if he might actually have meant it. And then the awkwardness afterward, where I wasn't sure if he'd really meant it and wanted an answer, or if he'd been joking.

I still didn't know.

One thing I did know? I didn't like the fact that his ex was trying to get him back, more than likely right now. He might think he wouldn't go running into her arms, but I knew how he thought. I knew his code of honor. If everyone expected him to forgive and forget, would he? Would he accept his ex-fiancée with open arms?

It's not as if he'd had his heart broken by her.

There was no emotional reason not to forgive her and have that lovely merger they'd both been planning on before she dropped her panties for another man.

It made me wonder what she looked like. She was probably classy and elegant. Buttoned up to the top button, pencil skirt to the knees, sensible black pumps. I looked at my jeans and sweater with black boots, my head tipped to the side, and tugged on the blue streak I'd put in my hair.

She'd probably never put blue in her hair.

Riley would more than likely love having a proper wife like her. One who might be questionable in virtue and honor, but who would look damn good on his arm.

Just the thought made me sick to my stomach.

Not good. Not good at *all*.

My chest tightened, and I stood shakily. After shooting Emily an apologetic look, I hurried for the doors. I felt like I couldn't breathe, or like I was going to vomit. Or both.

As soon as I came out the double doors, I gulped in some fresh air. It felt exactly the same as the air inside the room had felt in my lungs. Hot. Stale. Stagnant.

Stumbling toward the exit, I reached into my purse and pulled out my phone. I needed a second to clear my head. To figure out why the heck I felt as if I was about to panic or cry or vomit or whatever. To pull myself together.

The bright sun hit me hard, but the air…ah, that's what I'd needed. Fresh air. No one to bother me. No one to see me when I—

"Noelle?" Emily came up behind me, her heels clacking on the concrete. "Are you okay?"

I closed my eyes. I loved Emily to death, but I couldn't talk to her about this. I mean, she was Roger's sister. Even though Roger was gone, it still didn't feel right to sit and talk to her about how Riley had proposed to me while I had been going down on him. She might have been my best friend before she'd been my sister-in-law, but she'd been his sister first. And nothing would change that.

"I'm fine. It was just so hot in there," I said, forcing a laugh. "You know?"

"Yeah, it was."

I glanced away, uncomfortable with her piercing brown eyes on me. They looked so much like Roger's that it felt as if *he* was watching me. "You can go back in. I'll be fine alone for a few minutes."

"I just wanted to check on you." She lifted a foot, stepped back, and then stopped. "Did something happen? Maybe something to do with Riley?"

"I don't…I can't talk about it right now."

She pressed her lips together and nodded. "You know I don't mind, right?"

"I know." I looked at her, smiling as best as I could manage. "I do. But until I know what's going on, what's real and what's not, I'd rather just…not."

Her eyes focused somewhere over my shoulder. "Did last night end badly?"

"Not last night," I muttered under my breath.

She blinked at me. "What?"

"No, why?"

Her eyes went all wide, and then she backed off. "Uh, nothing. Never mind. I'll just…uh…go back in."

"Em, what's—?"

"I deserve better?" Riley asked from behind me, his voice gravelly and rough and sexy. Oh so freaking sexy. He had the type of voice that romance writers wrote about. Like, Benedict Cumberbatch sexy, only minus the English accent. Instead of detracting from the overall sexiness, though, it somehow made him even hotter. "That's what you said?"

I closed my eyes for a second before turning around to face him. He was all disheveled, with his hair sticking up in odd places, and he hadn't even buttoned his shirt all the way. Even so, he looked like a million bucks. It wasn't fair, because I felt like shit. "Yeah. I said that."

"Then don't walk out on me like that." He backed me up against the wall, placing a hand on either side of my head. The show of anger and dominance did weird things to my stomach. Big shocker there. "If you're going to say you're done with us, at least do it properly."

Before I could reply, his mouth was on mine, his hand was in my hair, and he was kissing me until I didn't want him to stop. Ever. As his mouth moved over mine, he slipped a knee in between my legs, brushing against my aching core with picture-perfect precision. I moaned into his mouth, and he deepened the kiss.

Right when I was ready to drag him back to my room with me, he broke it off, his breathing as ragged as mine. Dropping his forehead to mine, his fingers tightened on my hair. "That's how you say goodbye properly. I know I fucked up and scared you off with my proposal, but I didn't deserve a fucking note as a goodbye. I…I…"

Pushing off the wall, he walked away from me without finishing his sentence.

Just like that.

For a second, I watched him go, swallowing hard. I wanted to chase after him, but I knew I shouldn't. Logically speaking, it was best to end it now. Logically speaking, we were both a mess of emotions. But despite that, I wanted him to come back. I wanted to see if he'd meant that proposal.

I *needed* to know, logic be damned.

"Riley!" Stumbling forward, I pressed my fingers to my swollen lips and called out, "Wait!"

He stopped instantly, his fists at his sides, and turned around. His beautiful eyes were cautious, and it hurt to see that. I hadn't meant to do that to him. "What?"

"I'm sorry."

He closed his eyes. "There's nothing to be sorry for. If you want to be done after what I did, that's fine. I just didn't expect you to run when I was naked in the shower."

"I didn't mean it. I'm not done."

"Then why did you say you were?" He glanced over his shoulder. "Was it because of what I said? Did I scare you?"

"Well…yeah. I didn't exactly expect you to propose marriage to me while I was naked in bed, kneeling between your legs with my ass in the air." I cocked a brow at him. "But you did, and I panicked."

"And you ran. I didn't expect that."

I bit my lip. "So we both did the unexpected today, for better or for worse. Can we call it even?"

He studied me for a couple of seconds, and then burst into laughter. "Shit, you're killing me, Smalls."

Choking on a laugh, I cupped his face in my hands. "How so?"

"You just are." He kissed the tip of my nose, and smiled down at me. His eyes were no longer guarded, which made me all giddy and lightheaded like a schoolgirl. "About that note…"

I swallowed hard. "I didn't really want to say goodbye. I just kind of panicked."

"You're the second person to say that to me today," he muttered. "But the first I want to believe."

"What can I do to make it up to you?"

His eyes lit up. "Marry me. Right now."

"Riley…" My heart sped up traitorously. "You shouldn't joke around like that. Marriage is a serious thing."

"I'm dead fucking serious. Marry me."

If my heart had been racing before, it was now travelling at warp speed. "Why would you want to marry me? I don't even live here."

"We could change that, if you married me. Duh."

I choked on a laugh. "I kind of have a job across the country."

"What if you didn't need it?"

"I'd still want it." I dropped my hands to my sides. "What's really going on, Riley?"

"My mother is already lining up my next fiancée." He held his phone up. It was lit up with nonstop text messages from *Mom Cell*, as well as a few from *Carrie*. "She has five dates lined up for me in the next week. On top of that, Sarah is probably convinced I'll fall back into her arms, just like you said. And they both expect me to do whatever they want."

I crossed my arms. "And?"

"And I know what *I* want. I want the girl who expects me to do whatever the hell I want. I want the girl who finds the guy who has nowhere to go and offers him a bed." He tugged on his tie. "I want *you*. I want to marry you."

My heart stuttered to a stop. "That's…that's…*crazy*."

"But it's not. Not really." He grabbed my hands and kissed the knuckles. "I want to marry you because you make me be spontaneous and free, and I've never been like this. You make me a better me. The kind of me I almost was before I wasn't anymore. You brought that version of me back to life. If that makes sense."

I leaned in to him but forced myself to straighten, yanking my hands free. "It does. It really does. But this is a reason to *date* someone, not *marry* them."

He advanced on me, and I retreated until I hit the wall again. The rough brick dug into my back and my palms, but that wasn't what made my heart pick up speed. It was the man in front of me. Gripping my chin, he tipped it up and met my eyes.

"I like you, Noelle. A hell of a lot. You make me feel like maybe I have a chance, a real chance, at being happy. With you as my wife, I'd laugh. I'd live. I'd have fun. That's more than I can say for anyone else in this world."

For some reason, his twisted reasoning made complete sense. "I get that, I do. But—"

"No buts. Don't let logic in. Ignore it. Just concentrate on this." He ran his thumb over my jawline, making me shiver. "On us. That's what I'm doing, damn it. I don't want to be scared of taking a chance—not when it means I could lose you. Something is telling me with every fiber of my being that I need to marry you before you walk away forever."

My eyes filled with tears because he was saying all the right things and his tenderness and sincerity were melting my resolve to be rational. "Look, I like you a lot, too. I really do. But we barely know each other. We can't just get *married* like that."

"Why not? People do it all the time."

I laughed. "No. They don't."

"Okay, fine. You're right, which is exactly why we should do it. Let's be crazy and wild and free." He stepped back, his eyes lit up in determination. "Let's throw caution to the wind, and just fucking do it. Just say yes."

Man, he was making me want to say yes. I'd always lived my life so cautiously. Heck, it had taken me three weeks to answer Roger when he'd proposed to me, and I'd known him my whole life. But now Riley, a man I'd just met, was here, asking me to be silly and free and marry him on a whim. I couldn't do that, could I? "Riley…"

"Fine. But be warned: I'll keep asking until you decide we know each other well enough to say yes."

My heart melted. "You realize I'm leaving soon, right?"

"I'll convince you before then." He grinned. "I'm not worried."

"You're so sure?"

"Yep." He looked over his shoulder and smoothed his hair. "You know, I have a secret."

I shuffled my feet, because I had lots of them. "And it is…?"

"I'm rich." Leaning in, he whispered, "Really rich."

I snorted. "I already knew that, and I don't care about your money."

"That's one of the many things I like about you. I also love your laugh, your smile, your generosity, the way you moan when you're seconds from—"

I pressed my fingers to his mouth, my cheeks heating up. "Shh. Someone will hear you."

He cast an amused glance around. There was no one around us. "Shit. Don't tell me you see dead people like that kid in that movie?"

"What?" A bubble of laughter escaped me, and I shook my head. "You're crazy."

"I'm crazy?" He pointed to his chest with a ludicrous expression on his face. "You're the one who sees dead people all around us."

"Oh my God."

He lit up like a light bulb. "Oh, I like it when you moan that, too."

"*Riley.*"

"All right, all right. I have to get to work anyway." He tugged on his tie and met my eyes. "Where my gorgeous ex is probably still waiting for me. Feeling jealous yet?"

"Actually, yes." I glared at him. "Now I am."

He lifted his left hand and pointed at his ring finger. "If you liked it, then you should have put a ring on it."

Covering my mouth, I burst into laughter again. "You're incorrigible."

"Yep. Will you marry me yet?"

I shook my head, grinning like a demented fool. "Nope."

"Fine." Turning around, he lifted his arm and waved. "Till later then?"

Hugging myself, I nodded. I knew he couldn't see me, but I did it anyway. As I watched him leave, I had a sinking suspicion that I was fighting a losing battle. Something told me when Riley Stapleton set his mind on something…

He got it.

# chapter fourteen

## Riley

A couple of hours later, I sat back against my desk chair and rubbed my forehead. I'd been working without a break for way too fucking long, but I was determined to finish up and get the hell out of here as fast as I could. I had a girl to see, and I had to convince her to marry me.

Deep down, I knew I was going against every guy code ever written by pursuing her so voraciously, but I'd lived my life surrounded by two people who truly, fully loved one another. Carrie and Finn Coram. I'd watched them fall more and more in love every day they were together, and they'd been together for more than nine years now.

Even when I'd had a thing for her, I'd known nothing would ever actually come of it, because she and Finn had the kind of love that poets wrote about. A love that nothing, and no one, could destroy. They'd had so much shit thrown at them during the years, even as recently as a year ago, but they'd pulled through it even stronger than before.

I'd never fully believed I could get that in my life.

Didn't think I could find that kind of love for me. But the feeling I had in my chest? The one that grew tighter every time I walked away from Noelle, only to loosen the second I saw her? The one that told me to find her, drag her to the nearest courthouse, and marry her before she realized she could do better than me?

Yeah. I had a feeling that would turn into love.

And I wasn't losing my fucking chance at that because I was too scared to chase after it. I'd chase her until she accepted that we were meant to be. Unless she flat out told me to go away, I'd follow her to the other side of the country if need be. But she wouldn't. Despite her more rational approach, she felt it, too. I saw it in her eyes.

Reaching out, I grabbed the photo of Sarah and me off my desk and tossed it in the garbage. That chapter of my life was over. I was done doing things because people expected it of me. I was done being the good little son who did everything he was asked.

It was time to start being *me* again.

Pulling up the romance conference website, I scanned the pages till I found what I wanted. Someone knocked on the door, and I glanced up, my heartbeat picking up momentum. Had she come to see me again? The receptionist was under strict orders to let her in without question if she did. "Come in."

The door cracked open, and Carrie poked her red head in. "Hey. It's me."

"Oh, hey." I closed my computer, disappointment hitting me in the gut. I'd thought... "How's it going?"

"I'm fine." She opened the door more, and Finn followed her in. His light brown hair was curly and a little wild, and so was Carrie's. "But more importantly, how are you?"

I waved my hand dismissively. "I'm fine."

"But what about Sarah?" She glanced at Finn, who shrugged. "She cheated on you. That *sucks*."

"Yeah. I guess so, but it's over now. So it doesn't suck anymore." I leaned back in my chair and eyed them both. "Where were you two?"

"Surfing," Finn said, grinning. "She did awesome out there."

"Of course she did," I said.

"Stop changing the subject," Carrie snapped. "Shouldn't you be, I don't know, *upset*? On the phone last night, you sounded pretty calm, but I thought you were just putting on a good face or something."

I locked eyes with Finn, who stared back at me silently. His head was cocked, and he looked as if he was assessing me. "He's not upset because he didn't love her."

Carrie looked at him with wide eyes and turned to me. "Is this true?"

"Yeah." I looked at Finn again. His blue eyes were locked on me. "How did you know?"

"You basically admitted as much to me the night you came to see me in the hotel." He glanced at Carrie and threw his arm around her.

Something shadowed his eyes, and it didn't take much to figure out what. A lot had happened on that night. "It didn't take much to put two and two together after what you said."

"If you didn't love her," Carrie said, gripping Finn's hand tight for support, "why did you ask her to marry you?"

I watched them, my heart filled with happiness for my best friends. But this. Right here? It's what I wanted. What I had a feeling I could have with Noelle. It's why I couldn't be a pussy. It's why I had to make her see I was right. "Because it was expected of me, and she was nice."

Finn still stared at me.

Carrie smacked my arm. "You *idiot*."

"Ow." I rubbed my abused arm. "What? I didn't love anyone. I had no reason not to do it, so I did it to make everyone happy."

"Everyone except you."

I shrugged. "Whatever. Logically, it made sense for all parties involved to just go ahead and do it anyway."

"It made—" She went after me again, and Finn pulled her back.

"Easy there, slugger." Finn tossed his arms over her shoulders, holding her in place in front of him. "Let the man be."

She didn't fight his hold. Instead, she leaned against him. "Honestly, Riley, if the college-aged version of you could hear this, he'd punch you in the face."

"Probably." I grinned at Carrie. "But he'd have to catch me first."

Finn narrowed his eyes. "You're looking at her differently."

"What?" I asked, caught off guard. "What do you mean?"

"You always looked at Carrie like she was the epitome of the girl you'd like to have for yourself, and I let it go, because she's fucking perfect. I didn't blame you." Finn let go of Carrie and came behind my desk, walking around me with a finger pressed to his chin. "But now it's as if you've moved on from that. Why? What happened?"

Carrie flushed. "Finn, he never looked at me like—"

"Yeah, he did." Finn stopped in front of me. I fidgeted uneasily. "He wasn't going to try and steal you or anything, but he did look at you that way."

I glanced at Carrie, then back at Finn. "I may have…"

"Fine. Whatever. But you're not anymore?" Carrie flushed even more, not meeting my eyes. "Why?"

"He met someone," Finn called out, his blue eyes lighting up. Carrie, for her part, perked up like a dog who had been given a huge bone. "Someone he *likes*."

My cheeks heated. "Guys…"

"Who is she?" Finn asked. "Spill it, Stapleton."

"Do I know her?" Carrie asked, advancing on me.

I felt like a caged beast, desperate to get free. Pushing my chair back, I stood and held my hands up in surrender. "Seriously, guys, chill."

Carrie shook her head, those bright blue eyes of hers shining with excitement. Now, instead of getting mesmerized by them, I thought of another pair of eyes. Noelle's. "Tell me *everything.*"

I glanced at Finn. "Are you going to help me out here?"

"Nope. You're on your own, man." He crossed his arms. "Oh, shit. Is she the one-night-stand girl?"

Closing my eyes, I groaned. "*Finn.* What. The. Fuck?"

"You had a one-night stand?" Carrie asked, her eyes wide. "With *who?*"

"Shoot me. Shoot me now."

Finn snorted. "It totally is her. You didn't run, did you?"

I might as well stop fighting it. They wouldn't leave me alone until I gave them all the juicy details—minus the intimate ones, of course. "Actually, I did. But I left her some cash and my business card after I left, and she stormed into my office later that day."

Carrie's mouth dropped. "She's a...a...*hooker?*"

"Dude." Finn lowered his arms. "Your ego might have taken a blow and all, but I'm sure you could have found someone at least somewhat willing to fuck you without paying them for—"

Carrie smacked him this time. "Finn."

"She's not a hooker." I pinched the bridge of my nose and checked the time, knowing I'd have to tell them what they wanted to hear. Almost four o'clock. I wanted to be out of here soon, so I better get to it. "Sit down, and I'll tell you everything."

They exchanged a silent look, and then sat in front of my desk. I sat on the edge of it. "Okay, so here goes."

I told them everything, from the mishap with the money to her storming into my office to set me straight to last night. Knowing their knowledge of love might be a help to me, I even told them about this morning—minus what she'd been doing to me when I'd popped the question.

"You proposed? *Already?*" Carrie spluttered and sat up straight. "What did she say?"

"No, of course." I shrugged. "But I'll change her mind."

"Dude." Finn cleared his throat and glanced at Carrie before turning his piercing eyes back on me. "Don't you think this is all moving a little fast?"

I narrowed my eyes on him. "Have you ever known me to act irrationally or without thought?"

"No," he said.

Carrie shook her head and replied at the same time as her husband. "Never."

"This girl makes me feel...so much." I pressed a hand to my heart, meeting both of their eyes in turn. "I know, logically speaking, that I barely know her. But I've watched you two from the sidelines for a long time, knowing you had a love that would never die. I didn't think I would ever find a girl who made me want the same."

Finn nodded.

Carrie pressed a hand to her own heart. "And you think you found that in this girl? This Noelle?"

"I know when she leaves me I immediately start thinking about when I can see her again. I know I like everything about her, from her smile to the way she sleeps at night. She's kind and loving and doesn't give a damn about my money. If anything, it makes her dislike me a little bit." I stood up, pacing back and forth. "And I know I'll keep asking her to marry me until she says yes, no matter what anyone else says. I don't care what they think. For once in my life, I'm going to be crazy and wild and impulsive. I'm going to do something because I want to, not because I *have* to. I just need to get her to say yes."

Carrie's stared at me. Even Finn looked shocked.

I cleared my throat uncomfortably as they continued to stare at me without speaking. "Say something," I demanded. "You're creeping me out."

Carrie cleared her throat. "This is very sudden. Are you sure this isn't a reaction to what happened with Sarah? You shouldn't make life decisions after an emotional blow. It can throw off your reasoning. Make you feel things you don't really feel."

Finn sighed. "Ginger, sometimes all it takes is one look for a guy to know. I knew right away that I wanted to spend the rest of my life with you. I tried to fight it, but I knew."

"Yeah, the only difference is I'm not fighting it. I'm embracing it like it's my long-lost best friend."

"See? Our little boy is growing up," Finn said, grinning at Carrie.

She glanced at me. "He is. But still, I—"

"Just accept it for what it is, Ginger. He wants her, and he's going to get her. I did the same thing with you, if you recall." He kissed her nose. "We moved fast, too."

She sighed. "But still..."

"Jesus," I groaned, closing my eyes and fisting my hands. "Are you two going to help me woo her or not?"

Carrie pressed her lips together. "Your mother won't like you with a girl she didn't pick."

"Neither did yours at first. But now she loves Finn."

She smiled at Finn. "That's true."

"No offense, man, but your mom?" He ruffled his hair and stared at me from under his ducked head. "She's a little more hard core than Carrie's mom."

"Whatever." I shook my head. "I don't care."

Carrie pressed a finger to her lips. "Even if—?"

"Even if the sun falls out of the fucking sky, and the president himself asks me to reconsider my options." I locked gazes with Carrie. "I wouldn't give a damn. So. Are you in?" I included Finn in my stare down. "Or are you out?"

Finn and Carrie exchanged another one of those long, silent stares that said so much without a single word. Then they turned to me, grinned, and said in unison: "We're in."

I smiled and rubbed my hands together. "So, where do we start?"

# chapter fifteen

## Noelle

I walked out of the last panel of the day, rubbing my nose as I went. Emily walked beside me, jabbering on about something one of the panelists had said about BDSM that had pissed her off. I listened with half an ear, but the other half was focused on an idea that had popped in my head. The panel had sparked a plot bunny in my head, and it wouldn't stop hopping around like a maniac. I needed to get to a computer ASAP, before I forgot the details. There would be ropes, handcuffs, and a feather whip that would make the heroine—

Emily elbowed me, her eyes narrow. "Excuse me, are you listening to me at all?"

"Huh?" I blinked at her. "Uh, yeah. You're angry because BDSM isn't the way that chick portrayed it, though I'd love to know how you know that."

Emily flushed bright red. "Never mind that."

"There's no way in hell I'm never-minding that. You have to tell—"

"Noelle. *No.*"

I clamped my mouth shut. "Fine."

"About that talk, it was bullshit."

"I thought it was cool, though," I said, glancing at my phone. We had more than an hour until the next event, which was a party with free booze. "Are you going to the masquerade tonight?"

"Wouldn't miss it," Emily said, grinning. She was obviously relieved I'd let her whole I-know-all-about-BDSM thing slide...for now. "You have to come. Please tell me you're coming."

"Oh, I'm coming. I bought a mask for it and everything."

She grinned. "I bet you did. You always liked dressing up."

"That's because it was the one time no one could tell right away who I was." I lifted a shoulder. "I liked that."

"I know." She sighed and linked arms with me. "Did you meet up with that editor who wanted to buy your next series?"

"I did. We're still talking, but it looks promising." I smiled. "They want me to do a darker romance series. Like, antiheroes and all that. It'll be fun."

She whistled through her teeth. "Damn, that's different from billionaire CEO's. Are you ready for that?"

"I think everyone is," I said drily. "We can only deal with so many of those before they're annoying. My next hero is going to be a mechanic or something."

"Or a lawyer?" she asked, nudging me with her elbow.

"Hell no." I laughed. "Too close to home."

"Speaking of which…" Emily stole a quick glance at me. "Will Riley be there tonight?"

"I told him about it, but I doubt he's going to show up," I said, playing with the lanyard around my neck. "He doesn't have a ticket, after all."

Emily nodded seriously. "Yeah, because no one's ever crashed a party in the existence of humanity. Like, that would be *unheard* of."

"I highly doubt a lawyer is going to crash a romance author masquerade." I let go of the lanyard and exhaled. "I'm not holding my breath."

"Did something go wrong this morning? He looked awfully angry."

"No, it was great." I shook my head. "Fine."

I tucked my hair behind my ear and stopped at the elevator, pushing the buttons to my floor. Emily did the same. We both got assigned elevator C, so we walked over to it.

"Which one was it? Fine or great?"

"Aren't they the same thing?" I asked, even though I damn well knew they weren't. "Either one is good."

"They're not, and you know it."

Emily stepped onto the elevator when it opened.

I followed her on. No one else came on, which was a miracle.

The whole ride up, we stood there silently. And when she got off, I barely managed a halfhearted wave because I was so distracted by

Riley. He…he was just so alive. So impulsive and free and *fun*. He made me feel so alive, for the first time in more than a year and a half.

Was it wrong to feel so strong, so fast, when I'd lost the man I'd loved my whole life? Is that something I should feel wrong for?

The doors opened, and I walked off the elevator, my mind whirling in circles until I couldn't even see where I was going. I managed to unlock the door, then stepped into the silent hotel room. When I flicked the light on, the sight that met me was…

Unbelievable.

The whole room was covered in vases of gorgeous, fragrant flowers. Pink ones. Yellow ones. White ones. Roses. Tulips. Birds of paradise. If it existed in nature, it was *here*. On the bed, in one of those giant red envelopes that were bigger than me, was a card with my name on it. I didn't move, though. I was too busy staring at the greenhouse that was now my room.

Tears filled my eyes, and I sat down on the bed hard. This was…it was…too much. Riley was too much. He was fabulous and wonderful and romantic. This was crazy. He was crazy. And I was crazy about him.

If it was wrong to fall so hard and so fast, then I didn't want to be right. It might be a cliché to think that, but it was true. I didn't.

With a trembling hand, I swiped away the tears on my cheeks and grabbed the card. After ripping it open, I stared down at the card. The front said: *Thank You*. I opened it slowly, not sure what he was thanking me for. *For being you.*

I let out a small laugh. Underneath the print, Riley had written:

Pretty girls should have pretty flowers. I'll see you soon…but will it be before you see me?

—Riley

Smiling, I set the card down and stared at all the flowers. I headed for the shower with a huge smile on my face, stopping to smell the flowers along the way. By the time I was dressed, my legs were shaking with nerves. I'd put on a formfitting black dress. It was tight, and I tugged at it in an attempt to make it longer, but I knew it was fine the way it was. I'd been planning on forgoing the dress for a pair of pants and a glittery tank top, but if there was half a chance Riley would be there, I had to wear it.

Is that what his note had meant? That he would be coming to the ball?

If so, my resolve against him would melt further. I liked him, and if he kept begging me to throw caution to the wind and take him as mine, I just might do it.

He'd better watch out.

Slipping my red mask over my eyes, I surveyed myself in the mirror. My long blonde hair was curled and resting over my shoulders. My hazel eyes looked almost blue against the red mask, and I'd put on dark lipstick. The dress pushed my too-large breasts high, giving me that va-va-voom cleavage that I generally avoided.

I almost took it off. Almost went back to my comfortable jeans and tank. But Emily was right. I had to take chances. Have fun. *Live.* I'd bought the dress because Emily had said it looked good on me, and I'll be damned if I didn't wear it because I was scared to draw attention to myself. And that was that.

Nodding once, I picked up my stuff, cast one more glance at all the flowers, and headed out the door. The whole ride down in the elevator I fidgeted with my phone. Emily was waiting for me in the lobby, and then we were going inside the party.

The elevator doors opened and I stepped out. I saw Emily right away. She wore a sexy purple dress and black heels. She looked beautiful.

Her eyes widened from behind the purple mask she wore, and she whistled through her teeth. "Day-um, girl. You look hot."

Without replying, I walked up to her and hugged her close. For a second, she just stood there, but then she hugged me back. We stood there for a second like that, neither one of us speaking. When I pulled back, I looked into her eyes and whispered, "Thank you."

"Anytime, sis." Emily smiled, but her eyes looked sad. "Anytime."

"Ready to go dance," I offered her my elbow, "and get a little drunk? Because we have a lot to celebrate, you and I."

She linked arms with me. "You know it."

We entered the dark ballroom, disco lights whirling across the whole room in tune with the pumping music. I almost turned around and walked right back out, but I forced myself to stay. To not be the introvert that couldn't stand crowds tonight.

"Want a drink?" Emily shouted into my ear. I nodded, and she gave me a thumbs-up. "I'll get the first round. Be right back."

I nodded, watching her weave her way through the crowd. As I stood there alone, I scanned the crowded room for any sign of Riley. He was pretty tall, so mask or not, I had a feeling that I'd see his blond head before he saw me. Someone came up behind me, rested his hands on my shoulders, and pressed his body up to mine.

It was hard to hear his voice, even though I could tell he said something, but I only knew of one dude who would come up to me in a party like that and press his bulge against my butt. It had to be Riley. "You found me first."

Without turning around, I reached behind me and pulled him closer, cupping his butt with both of my hands. The second he pressed more fully against me, I froze. Riley was taller and thinner, with lean muscles that made my mouth water.

Not short and so big he could break a house.

"Yeah, I did," the dude behind me said. "I'm—"

"Not the guy I thought you were," I said quickly, letting go of him and twirling around. This guy looked nothing like Riley. He was a cover model. "I'm so sorry."

The guy, who was admittedly cute enough, grinned. I vaguely recognized him from one of the book covers I'd seen recently. He might be cute, but he wasn't Riley. So I wasn't interested. "Nothing to be sorry about."

"It was a mistake."

He stepped closer and touched my hair. "Want a drink, Ms. ...?"

"Mrs." I flashed my ring at him. I'd never been so happy to still be wearing it than I was now. I backed up a step. "So, no, thank you. I'm waiting for someone."

"I promise I won't bite." He followed me, reaching out to tug on the blue strand of my hair. "Hard."

I yanked my hair free. "No. I—"

Riley stepped between us, his tall frame slipping between the two of us. "The lady said no. Now fuck off."

The guy took one look at Riley, nodded, and left. Riley stood there for a second, his fists clenched at his sides, before turning around to face me. His black mask hugged his perfectly chiseled face to perfection, and the black button-up shirt rolled to his elbows was hot as hell. So were the black trousers that clung to every single inch of his body.

Every. Single. Inch.

But that impressive bulge against the seam of his zipper wasn't what caught my attention. No, the pure anger blazing in those bright green eyes of his was what had me standing motionless, barely daring to breathe. His shoulders were hard and straight, and I could feel the anger rolling off him in waves.

He looked as if he was ready to pummel the guy into the ground simply because he'd been talking to me. Flirting with me. That didn't make any sense. Riley wasn't the jealous type. Heck, he'd been more upset that his fiancée had slept with a dude on their couch than he had been about the actual cheating itself.

But right now he looked *pissed*.

# chapter

# sixteen

### Riley

I stood there under the disco lights, anger pulsing through my veins and turning my blood into an unfamiliar shade of green. I'd spent an hour trying to find the right outfit for this damn party of hers, not sure exactly what one wore to a masquerade party at a romance author's conference.

After I'd finally settled on an outfit after three unsuccessful tries, I'd realized I didn't own a mask. Why *would* I? I didn't exactly walk into the office wearing a different sequined mask over my eyes every day. So after a hurried visit to the party store, I'd found one. I'd wanted to meet her in her room and escort her down while telling her how gorgeous she looked.

Because she did. Look gorgeous. A lot.

But then I'd been late, and when I came inside the dark room, it had been just in time to see her grab some stranger's ass and pull him close. Funny thing was, in a crowd full of women and pulsating bodies, I'd found her within seconds of entering the room. I had a feeling that would always be the case, no matter how many years passed.

I couldn't enter a room and *not* see her instantly.

But I hadn't expected to walk in on her groping another dude. Just the mere sight of it, the memory of it, made me want to go all Hulk smash on the fucker.

"Riley?" Noelle said, her tone hesitant. "You okay?"

I shook my head slowly, not sure what this raw, ugly feeling coursing through me was. I wanted to...to... "Who was he?"

She blinked at me. "I have no idea. I think he was a cover model, though. I recognized him after..."

"So you grabbed his ass for fun or what?" I dragged my hand through my hair. "I thought you were different than that."

She flinched. "Are you even listening to yourself right now?"

"No. Not really. I just...*argh*."

I headed toward her, and she almost backed up, but then lifted her chin and stared me down. "You just what?"

Letting out an exasperated sigh, I curled my hand around the back of her neck, resting my thumb over her jawline. "I don't know. I just know I need to do this right now, before I fucking explode."

She blinked up at me. "Do what?"

"This."

I melded my mouth to hers, and all the tension in my shoulders magically faded away. For the first time all day, I could think clearly. I could see clearly.

And it was because of her.

Stepping closer, she let out a soft moan into my mouth, her small hands resting on my chest. It felt so right, so perfect, that I knew I wasn't insane for wanting this. For wanting her. This was real, and it was right, and I'd do anything to make her mine.

*Anything.*

I closed the distance between us and broke off the kiss, not wanting to be the guy who groped his girl in public. "I'm sorry. I don't know what that was."

"I think..." She peeked up at me. "I think that was jealousy?"

"But I don't—" I broke off, my cheeks heating. She was right. I'd totally been jealous. For the first time in my life, I'd experienced the big old green-eyed monster firsthand. "Get jealous. Fuck."

She laughed but covered her mouth. Her dancing hazel eyes stared up at me, and I wanted to kiss her again. Once. Twice. A million times. Whatever. "Have you seriously never been jealous?"

I thought about it. Even with Carrie, who I'd thought I'd loved, when she chose Finn, I'd kind of shrugged and accepted it. I hadn't had the blazing hunger and anger I had with Noelle. When I'd seen her kissing Finn all those years ago, I'd stood there and thought, *Well, that's it. Game over.*

But jealousy?

No. I didn't get that.

I shook my head. "Is that bad?"

"No." She dropped her hand from her mouth and entwined her fingers with mine. "I think it's adorable. But there was nothing between that guy and me."

"I know. I saw that," I muttered under my breath.

She smacked my arm. It made me want to kiss her again. I was sensing a trend here. "*Riley*. Seriously."

"I know. I'm sorry I said what I said. I know you're not like that." Leaning down, I kissed her temple, barely brushing my lips across her skin. We both shivered. "Forgive me?"

"Of course." She smiled up at me. "Thirsty?"

"Parched," I said, grinning back at her.

Her friend came up to us, three drinks in her hands. "Hey."

"Hey," Noelle said, her smile slipping away. She took a drink out of her friend's hand, handed one to me, and then took another for herself. "I don't think you two have been formally introduced. This is Riley. Riley, my best friend, Emily Brandt."

"Brandt?" I shook hands with her, smiling. "Wait, are you her sister?"

"Sister-in-law," Emily said. "But I loved her before my brother did, so I like to think of myself as her sister."

Before she finished speaking, I already felt like an ass.

*Oh…right. She wasn't her sister. She was her sister-in-law.* My gaze fell on the ring Noelle still wore. Some small part of me kept forgetting that Noelle had already been married. And she'd loved that man, actually *loved* him.

Enough to keep wearing his ring more than a year after he was gone.

No wonder she kept telling me no. I was a fool. Why would she want to marry me? She'd already had the real thing, and she'd never settle for anything less. I must look like such an idiot, asking her to marry me, and making speeches about having fun and doing what we wanted without thinking it through. Fucking *idiot*.

"Yes, of course," I said, letting go of her sister-in-law. "It's nice to meet you, officially."

"Back atcha," she said. She smiled at me, but it seemed reserved.

It made me wonder what she thought of Noelle and me. Like the last time I'd met her, I couldn't get a read on her. It must be painful, though, watching Noelle move on with a guy like me.

Had Noelle even done so, though? Had she really moved on?

It wasn't until now that I'd ever wavered in my certainty that she had to be as crazy about me as I was about her. What if I was wrong? What if I was the crazy dude who wouldn't take the hint? What if she didn't want me here?

I glanced at Noelle, who watched us both with not even a hint of a smile. And I needed some fresh air. I needed to…run. It was my turn. Clearing my throat, I finished my drink in one swallow and set it down. "You know what? You girls go have fun. I'm gonna head out."

"What?" Noelle glanced around the room. "You're leaving?"

Emily narrowed her eyes on me. "What's the rush, Captain?"

"No rush. It's just I…you…this is for…I'm…" I clamped my mouth shut and gave up on talking. I sounded like a fucking idiot, and felt like one, too. "I have to go."

Noelle watched me, but she didn't say anything.

Turning on my heel, I walked away. Underneath the booming music, I thought I heard Noelle and Emily arguing behind me, but I resisted the urge to turn and see if I was imagining things. As I walked to the double doors that led to freedom, I ripped my mask off and tossed it in the trash.

After the doors closed behind me, I leaned on the hotel wall and took a breath. I'd been interfering with her life in there, bursting into her party, and it hadn't felt good. I kept pushing and pushing to get closer to her, and maybe it was enough. Maybe it was time to take the hint and hit the road. Give up the fight.

Be like Elsa, and let it go.

Besides a few good fucks and a couple of stolen kisses, she'd never given me a reason to think she wanted more from me than what we'd had. And I wanted more. So much more. It hurt because in such a short time, she'd come to mean a lot to me. I knew it was fast and stupid and crazy, but I'd fallen for her, and I'd fallen hard.

But it seemed like she hadn't even tripped over me.

My heart wrenched sharply to the left, and I closed my eyes. All I saw swimming in the sea of blackness was her face. It haunted me. I had a feeling it always would, long after she'd forgotten all about me. The doors opened and I opened my eyes, not wanting to be caught moping around like a child who'd lost his favorite toy.

Noelle came stumbling out, her eyes scanning the room until she saw me. Then she marched over to me and crossed her arms. "What game are you playing?"

"I'm not." I stood up straight, swallowing hard. Fuck, even while ready to claw my eyes out, I wanted to hug her and kiss her and ask her to be mine. "I'm not playing games."

"It sure feels like you are." She bit down on her plump red lip, those hazel eyes I loved staring into my soul. "One second, you're begging me to marry you, sending nearly the entire contents of a greenhouse to my room, and being all adorable with jealousy. Then the *second* I start to think you have a point, and I should give in, you run away."

By the time she was finished, I couldn't draw in a breath. It felt like someone had punched a fist into my chest. "You were thinking about marrying me?"

"It's all I've been able to think about, you idiot." She curled her hands into balls at her sides. "Did you honestly think you asking me to marry you hasn't been on my mind? That I laughed it off and walked away, without a thought as to what I should say? What I should do?"

"Honestly, yes." I reached for her hands, but she pulled free. "You loved your husband. You're still wearing his ring."

"Yeah." She paled, twisting the ring I spoke of on her finger. "So?"

"I didn't want to cheapen that love you felt for him by telling you that you should marry me because I'm fun." I tugged at my shirtsleeves. "You've given me no reason to think that you might be interested in that at all. I don't even have your phone number, for fuck's sakes."

She blinked at me. "You want my phone number?"

"Yes, of course I do." I shook my head. "But that's not what I'm saying. I'm saying you had a real, true love, and now you're supposed to settle for me?"

"Settle? I wouldn't be settling for you."

I furrowed my brow. "Then why did you say no?"

"Because we don't really know each other. Because we live on separate sides of the country. Because you're you," she gestured at me, "and I'm me."

I cocked a brow. "Yeah...and...?"

"And I think your family would expect you to marry someone who isn't a widow who writes romance books, from what I've heard about them." When I opened my mouth to argue, she held her hand up. "*And*, as if that isn't bad enough, I'm not from the same background as you. Not even close. You have no idea how far apart we are on a scale of—"

"Seriously?" I eyed her as if I'd had no idea of this. I didn't give a shit about her lack of money, and she didn't give a shit about my overabundance. We were the perfect match. "Why didn't you tell me you weren't rich? This will never work."

Shaking her head, she said, "I'm serious."

"So am I." I dragged my hand through my hair. "I want you to be my wife. There is no doubt in my mind that we'd be happy together. I could spend the rest of my life trying to make you happy, and you'd make me the luckiest man in the world."

"You don't *really* want to marry me." She fidgeted and shook her head, but I swore I could sense her softening toward me. "I'm not the wife material you're looking for. Trust me. I'm not a trophy wife."

Rejection number three. It was time to give up. "I don't care about any of that shit, but I get that you're not interested." Rubbing the back of my neck, I forced a laugh even though I wanted to scream. "I mean, it's crazy, right?"

She laughed too. "It is."

"Marriage is serious. It's a big deal."

The laugh faded, and she twisted her ring again. "It is."

"And you don't want to marry me," I said, even though it hurt to say it out loud. Stupid, but true. It did. "I get it. I totally understand."

She opened her mouth and closed it. "Well..."

I nodded. "Right. So, I'll go. No hard feelings. It was stupid anyway. You were right to write me that note. To end it there, before things got weird. I should have listened to your advice and stayed away."

"I don't know about that," she said, smiling. It looked strained. "I do like you. A lot."

Walking past her, I kissed her temple as I went. "I like you a lot, too. Goodbye, my sweet Noelle."

She gripped my hand. "What if I had said yes? Would you have actually done it?"

"In a heartbeat."

"But why?" Her hazel eyes locked onto mine. "Why me?"

"I like you. For once in my life, I was thinking of myself instead of my parents, or my job...or anyone else. Just me and you."

She licked her red lips. "But—"

"No. That's it. That's all there is. No buts. No ands. You make me happy, and long ago, I swore if I found the woman who made me feel this way? As if I could do anything or be anyone? The one who made my heart race every time she smiled, laughed, or kissed me?" I pressed a hand over her heart, my own racing in response. "If I found the girl who could make this come to life within me? I'd marry her."

Tears filled her eyes, and she pressed a hand over mine, holding my palm more securely to her chest. "I do all those things to you already?"

"And more." I flipped my hand over and entwined my fingers with her. "So much fucking more. Noelle, I think I've fallen for you. If I haven't yet, then I will. I would fall so fucking hard. It's stupid and it's fast and it's hopeless, because you still love your husband, but I think I could love you, if you gave me the chance."

Tears spilled out of her eyes and down her cheeks. "You do?"

"I do." I took a shaky breath. "I didn't really recognize the feeling at first, since I've never really felt it, but I do. You're right, I am capable of love. And even though I barely know you, I just know I could love you the way you deserve to be loved."

She closed her eyes and took a shaky breath. "Riley..."

"I know. You don't have to say it."

"Say what?"

"No." I forced a smile even though it hurt. "You already said it three times. I don't need to hear it a fourth."

"Your mom would hate me," she said.

"I wouldn't care, but I think she'd love you." I paused. "Eventually." I paused again. "Maybe."

"Even if she didn't, you'd just…marry me anyway?"

"If you'd have me?" I nodded. "Yep. I would."

"Just like that?"

"Just like that."

She stared at me, her chest heaving beneath my fingers. I held still because I had a feeling we were on the verge of something huge here. Something that would change every single thing in my life. *Everything*.

"Two-one-two, five-five-five, six-four-three-two."

I blinked at her. "Huh?"

"That's my phone number."

A laugh escaped me. "Okay. Uh. Thanks?"

"And my birthday is May twentieth."

My heart pounded against my chest. "Mine's July sixteenth."

"I like dark chocolate better than milk."

"Me too," I replied. "Milk is washed down and gross."

"My favorite flowers are tulips. Any color. They smell good."

"They do," I agreed, confused as fuck.

"And I wear white gold or platinum. Not yellow."

My heart sped up. "Why are you telling me all this?"

"It's stuff you should know about your wife. Right?"

Everything froze. Her. Me. The people around us. "Are you saying…?"

"Ask me again," she whispered.

"Noelle…"

"Go on." She smiled at me, and my world shattered into a million pieces, only to be put back together all over again. This time, though, it was prettier and better and perfect. It was crystal clear and it smelled like heaven, all because of her. "Ask."

My throat dried out. "I don't have a ring."

"I don't care about that."

Squeezing her hand, I looked deep into those eyes of hers, the ones I loved so damn much, and asked, "Noelle Brandt, will you marry me?"

"Yes," she whispered. "God help us, yes, I will."

I picked her up, swung her in my arms, and kissed her. Right there, in front of anyone who was watching, I kissed her. And it felt fucking fabulous.

There was no doubt in my mind that this was it.

This was *love*.

# chapter

# seventeen

### Noelle

The next morning, I lay in bed watching Riley sleep. Last night had been a blur of craziness, and I had a feeling my life was about to get even crazier. Even though I'd agreed to marry him, it didn't feel real yet. But it would, because we had to actually *tell* people now. Like, his mother and Emily and the world.

God, what was I thinking? In what world was this okay? We would be ripped apart. Crucified, and with good cause. No one married each other after days of knowing each other. This wasn't realistically possible. It was crazy and stupid and... *Right*.

Oh so right.

I was sick of being scared to take a chance. I wanted to take a chance on Riley, and I was. I was totally going to do it. Even though it scared the crap outta me. And made no sense. At all. But I was doing it anyway. How could that possibly end badly?

Yeah. Sure. It would all go splendidly.

Moaning, I closed my eyes and forced a calming breath. I might be worried about what the rest of the world would think about our whirlwind marriage, but deep down, underneath all the worries and a heavy dose of reality...

Was the certainty that this was perfect.

Riley said the sweetest things, and did the sweetest things, and he made me happy. I'd been miserable for way too long already, so I was going to grab that happiness and hold on to it for dear life. Isn't that all anyone wanted out of life? Happiness?

Surely people would see that we made sense together.

Riley made a small noise, blinking against the sunlight. I watched him, smiling when he rubbed his eyes and yawned. As soon as he finished, he turned my way, his gaze scanning my face. "Good morning."

I smiled. "Good morning."

"You didn't run?"

"Nope." Reaching out, I brushed a lock of blond hair off his forehead. "Were you hoping I did?"

"No, then I'd have to chase you." He pulled me into his arms and kissed me. "And I don't like running. It's very undignified."

Snorting, I rolled my eyes. "Snob."

"Never." He tugged on my hair. "Are you busy tonight?"

I thought over my schedule. "No, why?"

"I was thinking of having a small dinner party. We could have a few friends there, and I could introduce you to my mom…"

I bit down on my tongue. "Oh, God. Already?"

"You said that last night a few times, too."

I buried my face in my pillow. If only I could hide from the rest of the world so easily. "I can't meet her yet. She's going to hate me."

"She's not *that* bad."

I narrowed my eyes at him. "Yeah, she is. I know it. She's going to hate me."

"But *I* don't and that's all that matters, right?" He cupped my cheek, those green eyes of his shining up at me like priceless emeralds. "You have my protection, Noelle. Against anyone or anything, including my mother. Who cares what anyone else thinks? All that matters is *us*. This." He kissed me gently, just a tender brushing of our lips. "I'm yours, and you're mine. That's all that matters, now or ever."

My heart melted into a tiny little puddle, and so did my panties. "You say all the right things at all the right times."

"It's a gift," he said, grinning up at me. "I plan on abusing it fairly often during the next fifty years or so. Let's get married."

I blinked down at him. "I already said I would. You don't have to ask me again."

"No. I mean, right now." He sat up, and I scrambled back to sit down before I fell off the bed. "I don't want to wait another second to marry you. I want you to be mine now. Forever. Marry me. Today."

My heart fluttered. "Every time you ask me that, my stomach does flip-flops that steal my breath away."

"I plan to steal your breath away every day for the rest of our lives." He bent down, locking eyes with me. "Let me. Let's go get married."

"It's not that easy, is it? I mean, we need a license and papers...and an officiate."

"I might have already applied for them after I asked you the first time and pushed them through quickly." He flushed a little bit. "And I know a guy. Marry me."

I laughed, but inside my body was screaming *yes, yes, yes!* "Are you sure you want to do this?"

"Yes." He brushed his fingers over my pulse, sending it scattering even faster. "Are you? Because if you're not, we can wait."

Silently, I studied him, unable to speak. This man, this unbelievably attractive, kind, loving man wanted to marry me within days of meeting me. If someone had told me last week that I'd meet a man in a hotel, invite him up to my room sight unseen, and then marry him days later, I'd have throat punched them and had them committed.

But now, it made total and complete sense.

Weird how life worked like that.

Smiling, I nodded. "I'm sure, yes. I just don't want people to think I rushed you to the altar."

"I think it's the other way around."

"In all reality, yes." I shrugged. "But they'll always think it was me. Speaking of which, we need a prenup."

"No." He pushed back, frowning down at me. "Absolutely not."

Biting my lip, I rolled over and grabbed a napkin off the nightstand, and a pen. "Yes, we do, and you know it. You're rich."

"You said you don't care about that..."

"I don't. But everyone else does." Scribbling down a quick sentence, I handed the napkin to him. "Which is why we need it."

"But—" He glanced down at the napkin, his knuckles going white. "'I, Noelle Brandt, solemnly swear the only thing I want from Riley Stapleton out of our marriage is his heart.'"

I held the pen out. "Sign it, so it's official."

"Noelle..." He took the pen and scribbled his name down, then tossed it aside with the prenup. "You already have it, you know. You have my heart."

And then he kissed me, stealing away anything I would have said. He crawled over my body, pressing me back until I lay on the mattress again. He insinuated himself between my legs, his hard erection rubbing up against me. I certainly didn't mind, because I needed him now more than ever.

My stomach clenched and I wrapped my legs around him. "How are you so freaking awesome?"

"I'm not," he whispered, his mouth kissing a hot path down my neck. "I just know what I want. And when I want something, I'm insatiable." He slid in, and my breath hitched in my throat, but he stopped before entering me fully. "I need you, Noelle. Take me."

Nodding, I wrapped my arms around his neck. "Yes, I'll marry you today. Tomorrow. Next year. Whenever you want, as many times as you want."

He thrust into me all the way. "Today." He slid his hand down my leg and hauled me closer. "You're mine, Noelle. All mine."

His grip was domineering. Possessive. I knew then, in that moment, that he was right. That's why we made sense, even though we didn't. Even if my mind rebelled at the thought, my body knew the truth. I was his in every way. His mouth closed over mine, and he moaned deep in his throat. The things that sound did to me…

I'd never known anything else like it.

He moved, nothing separating us from one another, and that was okay. I was on the pill, and he was about to be my husband.

My freaking *husband*.

His tongue touched mine, and I dug my nails into his shoulders, the pressure building up faster and faster until I couldn't breathe. Couldn't think. All I could do was feel, and it was amazing. Everything about Riley was perfect. And when I was with him…for the first time in my life, I almost felt perfect, too.

Imagine that.

Framing my face with his hands, he thrust harder, his hips rolling with perfect precision as he kissed me. I clung to him, giving myself over to him. No more doubt. No more fears. If he could be so sure that we would work, then I could be, too.

Damn the rest of the world.

Sliding my hands down his back, I dug my heels into his ass, my hands dipping down to caress his skin. He shuddered and broke the kiss off, his breathing harsh and sexy as hell. "Jesus, Noelle. You feel so fucking good."

"You're the one who makes me feel like this." I dug my fingers into his back, arching my neck and groaning when he thrust even harder. His hard arms flexed, his sinewy muscles seducing me without even trying. "Only you."

"Yes." He kissed me again, not taking his mouth off mine as he whispered, "Only you."

Lowering his hand between us, he pressed his fingers against my throbbing clit, his hips going faster and harder and *oh my God*. I bit down on his lip, my entire body straining for the pleasure I knew he could give me. The pleasure only he could give me, the way he did it. When

I came, the whole world around us blurred into an unrecognizable tangle of lines and blobs and feelings until I forgot what my name was.

He thrust one more time, his body tensing as he came forcefully. With a strangled groan, he dropped his forehead on mine. "Noelle... Christ."

I nodded. "Yeah. That."

Laughing under his breath, he pulled back and stared down at me with the softest look in his eyes. If he kept stealing my breath away like this, I'd be dead before we made it to the altar. "You ready to make an honest man of me?"

"I am." Reaching up, I smoothed a lock of hair off his forehead. "I don't have a white dress, though."

He looked down at me with a sparkle in his eye. "That's okay, neither do I."

"Smart-ass." I smacked his arm. "You know what I mean."

"If you want a dress, we'll get you a dress."

"Let me tell Emily."

He kissed my nose. "Okay, I'll go shower while you do that."

After he left, I took a deep breath and picked up my phone. I knew she'd be happy for me, of course. But still, it felt weird to tell her I was marrying a guy I'd just met. Thinking about telling other people, and imagining their reactions, made it seem...foolish. Rash. And I didn't want to feel that way.

I wanted to be foolish and rash, darn it.

Quickly, I dialed her number before I could change my mind. It rang five times before going to voicemail. "Hey, it's me. Noelle. I...I'm doing it. We made a pinky promise that I wouldn't let happiness slip away, and with Riley...I'm happy. So happy, Em. So...I'm going to grab on to that happiness with both hands. He asked me to marry him, and I said yes. It's crazy, I know, but I hope, even so, that we have your blessing. We're going to go to the courthouse today to do it, and I hope you come. I want you there." I paused. "Please. Come. I'll text you the time later. I love you, Em."

With a muttered curse, I hung up. Riley came out, a damp towel wrapped around his waist. "How did it go?"

"She didn't answer." I tossed the phone aside. "I left a message asking her to come to the wedding."

"I bet she'll come." He pulled me to my feet and hugged me. I wrapped my arms around his neck. "She loves you, and she will be happy for you. I have no doubt."

I smiled up at him. "We're seriously doing this?"

"We're seriously doing this." He kissed my forehead. "We have a napkin prenup. No going back now."

"Where will we live?"

He smiled. "I'd prefer to live here, because my family is kind of all here, but if you want to go to New York instead, I'll follow you. I'll follow you wherever you want to go."

My heart swelled. I played with his hair and pursed my lips playfully. "I could maybe live in California...with the right persuasion."

After lots of kissing, laughing, and *persuasion*, I showered, and then we walked out of the hotel hand in hand, ignoring the real world and everyone in it for our little bubble of happiness. As we strode down the street, he stopped in front of a jeweler. It boasted unique wedding rings, and from the look of it, the price reflected as much.

The set in the window that caught my attention didn't have a price tag on it, but I could guess it was way too much for my blood. It had a big, brilliant white diamond in the center, and then diamonds circled the band all the way through. The diamond in the center had a circle of smaller diamonds around it, and it practically blinded me with its beauty.

I tore my eyes off the gorgeous set to see him staring at me. When I looked at him, he smiled. "You like that one?"

"I think every woman in the world would like that ring." I glanced at it again. "But it's too much."

"Why's it too much?" He looked back at it, confused. "Too gaudy for your tastes?"

"Too much *money*." I glanced down at the simple gold band Roger had given me. My thumb pressed against the back unconsciously, and I swallowed hard. I'd have to take it off. "I don't even really need a ring. It's fine."

His gaze dipped down to my wedding ring finger. The bright sparkle that was always in his eyes died away a little, and he slipped his shades up on his nose. "Yeah, you do. And so do I."

Without another word, he tugged me into the store behind him. The clerk stood when we came in, his eyes slipping past me and landing on Riley with greed. "Good morning. How can I help you?"

"Do you have any rings that would fit my lovely fiancée?" He held my right hand out. I tucked the left one behind my back. "We're madly in love and want to elope today, but we want to do it right."

The man pulled out one of those finger measures, slipped it over my finger, and nodded once. "It just so happens the set in the window out there would fit. It was a custom order, but unfortunately, the marriage fell through. It's quite a costly set, though."

Riley nodded once. "Bring it to us."

"Right away, sir," the clerk said. He practically ran to the window, and I shuffled my feet. "It will look lovely on the lady, if I may say so myself."

"Riley, you don't need to buy me fancy rings to make me happy. I just want you, like the napkin said," I whispered. "It's too much."

"Nothing's too much. Not when it comes to you." He didn't meet my eyes, but instead wandered over to the display with men's rings. "Do you happen to have one in my size as well?"

The man came up in front of me and set the ring down. "I'll check, sir." He turned the ring every which way, letting it sparkle and shine. It wasn't necessary. The beauty spoke all on its own without any silly sales theatrics. "But first…if I may…?"

My breath latched in my throat for the millionth time, and I slipped both hands behind my back. With little effort, I removed my wedding ring, fisted it in my right hand, and held out the proper hand. "Ahhh…perfect."

He slid it onto my finger, and he was right. It fit perfectly on me. I pressed my fisted hand to my heart, looking down at the ring with tears in my eyes. It was all too much. Too pretty. Too real. Too gorgeous to be real.

In a way, the ring represented Riley and me.

We were too perfect to be real, and yet here we were. Buying a ring. If there was a ring that encompassed what Riley and I were, this was it. "It's…it's…."

Riley came up beside me, his arm brushing mine as he stopped directly beside me. When he saw I'd removed my other wedding ring, he stiffened and glanced at me, his eyes wide. "Beautiful, just like you. We'll take it." He paused, ducking his head slightly. "If you like it, that is? I know it's different from…you know."

Not trusting myself to speak, I nodded.

"Then it's yours." He rested a hand on the small of my back, his touch claiming me as his more than a ring ever would. "Box it up, please."

The man clapped his hands. "Excellent. And now for you, sir…"

We walked over to the case with men's rings, and I watched silently as Riley got measured. Within seconds, the man announced he just "happened" to have a ring for Riley, too. Riley shot me a sardonic smile, but he took the ring out of the man's hands with no sign of hesitance. I caught his hand and took the ring from him. "Let me."

He stilled, his fingers tightening on mine. "As you wish."

Without glancing away, I slid the ring on his finger with a trembling hand. He swallowed hard, his own hand steady. It was white gold like mine, and it had a thin line of black throughout it with an elegant, scrawling gold design.

The ring fit as if it was made for him.

I smiled up at him, my heart fluttering madly. "Look at that, it's a perfect fit."

He caught my fingers, not letting go. Slowly, he opened my fisted hand and took out the gold band I'd hidden away. "Are you ready for this?"

Pressing my lips together, I knew I was. Against all rhyme or reason I was. "Yes. Let's do this."

A relieved grin lit up his face, and he handed it back to me. I slipped it into my purse and removed the ring on my finger, setting it next to his wedding band. As the jeweler boxed them up, I wandered off, hugging my arms close to my chest. I looked out the window, watching the way the sun popped through the clouds, shining down on the streets.

That's kind of how Riley had come into my life. It had been dark and gloomy and still, but then he'd shown up. I'd invited him into my room, and everything had changed. Pulling my phone out, I checked for any missed calls from Emily.

Nothing.

I shot her a quick text with the time and place of the wedding, then quickly put my phone away. He came up behind me and wrapped his arms around me, resting his chin on my head. "Whatcha thinking?"

I licked my lips. "That it's a pretty day for a wedding."

"Yes, it is." Letting go of me, he opened the door and offered me a small smile. "So let's go get you that dress."

I walked by him, my heart pounding in my chest as I passed him.

We were really going to do this.

Get *married*.

# chapter eighteen

## Riley

I stood at the makeshift altar in the courthouse, fidgeting with my suit as I waited. I hadn't seen Noelle since I'd dropped her off at the store, because she'd insisted I not see the dress until she walked down the aisle. Some small part of me was sure that this insistence was her way to escape before she had to marry me.

That annoying voice in the back of my head wouldn't shut up. It kept saying she'd never show up. I was going to be left at the altar, and I better accept that. Cursing under my breath, I checked my Rolex for what had to be the millionth time.

She was five minutes late.

That little voice in the back of my head was probably right. She was on a plane for New York right now, laughing under her breath because I'd fallen for her trick like the fool I was, and thanking God that she'd managed to escape me.

But that couldn't be true. She liked me. She didn't even know I was the son of the possible future vice president, but she liked me anyway. Patting the rings in my pocket, I paced back and forth. Would she still like me when she found out, or would she be unhappy? Maybe she would like me even more. Most girls did, but she wasn't most girls.

It's one of the things I liked about her so much.

I knew why I wanted to marry her, but why was *she* marrying *me*?

Aside from a boatload of cash, which she claimed not to give a shit about, I had nothing to offer her but me. And that had never been enough for anyone else.

Why would it be enough for a woman like Noelle?

Just as I was about to storm off the altar, the doors opened, and in came everything I'd ever hoped for, and more. As soon as I saw her standing there, wearing an off-white gown that fell to the floor, my heart stopped. Literally stopped.

She was going to be the death of me.

Once I remembered how to breathe, my heart raced with loud thuds echoing in my ears, and I took an unsteady step toward her. When she saw me, her eyes lit up and she smiled. It was then, in that moment, that I knew I wasn't going to fall in love with her. I couldn't fall in love with her, because I'd fallen in love with her the second I'd seen her in that hotel, waiting for the elevators.

It's why I'd talked to her that night, knowing damn well she wasn't going to check out. There had been this invisible pull between the two of us, and even drunk off my ass, I'd felt it. Thank God, because I was never going to let her go.

I wouldn't be the guy who went into the store and didn't talk to the girl.

This was what I'd wanted, all my life, and I had no doubt she felt the same way. If she didn't, she wouldn't be here now, wearing a white dress...

About to be *mine*.

"Emily?"

She shook her head, looking sad. "I can't find her, or get a hold of her. I think she's upset."

"Oh." Even though it killed me to ask it, I opened my mouth and asked, "Want to wait? Try to smooth things out?"

She shook her head.

I stalked down the aisle toward her, and she watched me with wide eyes. When I reached her, I stopped and flipped her veil over her head. She cocked her head and said, "What are you doing? You're not supposed to—"

"I don't give a damn. We haven't done anything right yet, so why start now?" I looked at the judge, who watched us with narrowed eyes. "We don't need any fancy words. Ask me."

"Do you take this woman, as your wedded wife, to have and to—"

"Yes." Tilting her face up to mine, I locked gazes with her again. Her bright hazel eyes pierced through my soul, taking a piece of me I'd never get back. "I take her, and swear to love her forever, until the day I die. Till death do us part."

She drew in a swift breath, her eyes filling up with tears. "Riley…"

"And do you take this man as your lawfully wedded—"

She nodded frantically. "Yes. So much yes."

The judge sighed. "Then with the power invested in me by the state of California, I now pronounce you husband and wife. You may kiss the—"

Grinning, I cut off the judge again. "I'm on it."

Without another word, I kissed her.

I kissed my *wife*.

My heart exploded into a flurry of beats, and her soft lips parted under mine. She tasted like happiness and heaven. Silly as fuck, I know. But it was true. She did. Her hands curled into the lapels of my jacket, and she leaned into me. She smelled like vanilla and was softer than satin…

And she was mine. All *mine*.

I broke off the kiss and grinned, resting my forehead on hers. "Hello, Mrs. Stapleton."

"Hello, husband." She rested her hands on my chest and laughed. "Oh my God. This is crazy."

"Absolute insanity."

"Everyone is going to kill us."

"Nah." I kissed her one more time. "I'll keep you safe."

The judge cleared his throat. "I need you to sign the papers to make it official."

As we signed, I kept stealing glances at her. Her hand trembled, but she signed the papers without any show of second-guessing herself. When we were all finished, the judge left us alone in the room with our marriage certificate.

She peeked up at me, and then averted her eyes. Wringing her hands in front of her stomach, she asked, "Did you tell anyone about this?"

"No." I scratched my head. "I'm going to tell them all at the dinner tonight. Why?"

"Emily," she whispered. "I hope she forgives me…"

"I'm sure she will. I doubt she's even mad. Maybe she's just… surprised. We both were, too." I hugged her close. I didn't want to face the real world yet. "Want me to go with you to find her?"

"Uh…" She tensed. "No. I think it's something I should do alone."

I reluctantly let her go. "Okay." I had a feeling if I let her leave, she would never come back. I also had the sinking suspicion I'd never get over that fear. Was this what love was? A crippling fear of losing the very thing you cherished. If so, I was in for a rough life. "Let me know if you need anything."

"Oh, don't worry." She rose up on tiptoe and kissed me. "I will."

Her lips lingered as if she didn't want to stop, or maybe it was mine.

Whatever. It felt fucking amazing either way.

"I don't want to let you go," I moaned, my hands flexing on her hips. "We should be on a flight to Maui or something right now."

She laughed. "We can have a delayed honeymoon. After we figure out the move, and what we're going to do."

And after I told her who my father was.

But first, we had to survive my *mother*.

"You're really okay with moving here, with me? If not, then—"

She placed a finger on my lips. "If I'm not okay with something, I assure you, I'll let you know—loudly and clearly. Don't you worry about that."

Smirking, I said, "Deal. And you can have whatever honeymoon you want, anywhere you want to go," I whispered against her lips. As long as we got one, I didn't give a damn where or when it happened. But I had this irrational fear it wouldn't happen. That as soon as she walked away, she'd come to her senses and leave. It wasn't as if she loved me or anything. "Anywhere in the world. It's all yours."

She frowned at me. "Stop throwing your money at me. I didn't marry you so you'd take me anywhere I wanted to go. I married you because you made me see where I wanted to be was with you. I think I need to have that prenup framed and hung on our wall."

I wanted to shout to the sky that I loved her. That I loved her, and nothing and no one would ever take that away from me. Now I just needed to make her love me, too. "You're amazing. You know that, right? You've been nothing but honest with me, and you have no idea how much I appreciate that."

"Yeah, I know. Same to you." She backed up a step, gripping her wedding dress in a death grip and mangling it in her fists. Suddenly, she didn't look so peaceful and happy. "Do you have to, uh, work today?" she asked.

"I do. Or, I did. I had a meeting scheduled for twelve. But if you want, I can make some excuses. We could go out to brunch, have a few mimosas, head back to the hotel…?"

"N-No." She shook her head, still wringing her dress. "Don't cancel for me. Treat this as a real day. Any normal, average day."

"All right." If she gave me even the slightest hint that she wanted to be with me, I'd cancel it. It wasn't a *real* day. It was our wedding day, and she was acting as if she already regretted it. "I'll be done in time for the dinner, though."

She paled even more. "Right. Where will it be?"

"I'll choose a place, and I'll pick you up at five." I hauled her against my chest, and she melted into me. Thank God. "Then the wedding night shall commence."

For the first time since I'd let go of her, she didn't look terrified. "All right. See you at five?"

"I'll be there." As she walked toward the door, I took a step toward her, my heartbeat echoing in my ears. *"Wait."*

She spun around, her plump red lips parted. "Yeah?"

Backing her against the wall, I kissed her with every single emotion I had whirling through my veins. Love. Lust. Fear. Hope. All of them mingled into that one kiss, and she clung to me for dear life. By the time I pulled back, she was breathless and her breasts rose and fell rapidly.

I slipped my hand under her ass, caressing her. If felt suspiciously smooth under that clinging satin. "What are you wearing under that dress, Mrs. Stapleton?"

Her cheeks pinked. "Nothing at all."

"Shit." I dropped my forehead on hers. "You're killing me, Smalls."

She chuckled and trailed her fingers down my chest. "I'll keep wearing nothing underneath my clothes today, if you'd like. All day long."

Like? I'd probably kill an entire army just to have the chance to see that. "I'd like that very much."

"All right." Letting go of me, she wiggled her fingers. She finally looked a little less worried and a little more flushed. "See you at five."

"I'll be there."

After one last longing look exchanged between us, she turned on her heel and walked away, white dress and all. This was so fucking fucked up, really. We were married, and all my dreams had come true, and I was supposed to go back to work as if nothing had happened?

It didn't make any sense. None of this did.

I should call into work and tell them to go fuck themselves, follow my wife, and take her back to our room so we could make love all afternoon long, like real couples did.

My phone vibrated, and I pulled it out. "Hello?"

"Where are you? I'm at your office," my mom said, her tone hard. "And you aren't."

"I'm coming in. I had…" I swallowed. "Something to take care of."

"What's more important than work?"

"Mom."

She huffed. "Never mind. I'll just have to see you later."

"About that. I want to have a little dinner party at the Boyd House. Intimate. Small." I took a deep breath. "How's six sound?"

"That sounds *perfect.*"

That went easier than I'd thought. I'd thought she would ask me a million questions about why I wanted to have a gathering, but she'd just accepted it. Maybe today was my lucky day. First, I'd married the girl of my dreams. Now this.

Nothing could stop me now.

"Great, I'll see you then."

"I can't *wait*," Mom said.

I hung up, a grin on my face. As I walked out the door, certificate in hand, I called Finn. He answered on the first ring. "Talk to me."

"I did it."

Finn shuffled the phone to the other hand. Or at least, it sounded like he had. "You did what, exactly?"

"I got her to say yes."

Finn laughed. "It was the flowers, wasn't it? Flowers always worked on Carrie."

"I think that helped, yes."

"Or maybe it was Carrie's idea of surprising her at the party." Finn paused. "Nah, I don't think so. It was definitely the flowers. You can thank me by making me your best man at your wedding. I look excellent in black."

"Um...about that?" I grinned even wider. "I kind of already married her."

Finn choked, then proceeded to cough for a good fifteen seconds. I swear my smile grew even wider with each passing second. I didn't often get the chance to catch him off guard like that. When he could speak again, he croaked, "Seriously? Already?"

"Yep. I convinced her and she said yes." I glanced down at my ring, rotating my hand and getting even happier. I was like a fucking giddy teenaged boy, but I didn't give a damn. "I got a ring and everything."

"Jesus, you weren't fucking around, were you?" Finn whistled through his teeth. "You actually did it?"

I dropped my hand. "Yep, and you two need to come to dinner tonight to be my buffers. I'm going to introduce her to Mom."

"Shit." Finn laughed. "You're going to need more than just us. You're going to need a fucking army. Do you think it would be better to tell her first, and give her time to adjust?"

"No, I think it'll be better in person. Once she meets Noelle, she'll love her. How could she not?"

Finn cleared his throat. "Riley, I never claimed to understand women, like, at all, but something tells me that's a bad plan."

I stiffened. There went the real world trying to drag me down already. "It'll be fine. Noelle is contagiously adorable. You can't help but love her. I would know."

Finn sighed. "Yeah, but you're a dude. Not an overprotective mother who wants to control every aspect of her son's life."

"Yeah, well, she can't." I gripped the phone tight. "And it's time she accepted that. I should have set her straight from the beginning."

"Well, if you need help, you can ask Carrie. She sure didn't have any issues with that when it came to me," Finn said, love shining through in his tone. It made me wonder if that was how I sounded when I talked about Noelle. "If you're sure it's how you want to tell her, you know I have your back. What time and where?"

"Boyd House at six."

"We'll be there, man." Finn clucked his tongue. "Call Carrie and fill her in."

I crossed the road to my Rolls-Royce. "Will do."

"And Riley?"

I settled into the seat and closed the door. "Yeah?"

"I'm very happy for you. I hope everything goes as planned tonight." Finn cleared his throat. "But in case it doesn't? Have an exit strategy in place. Always have an exit strategy in mind when going into hostile territory."

My heart sped up. "Copy that."

We hung up, and I sat there for a minute, staring at the people passing by. There were couples holding hands, smiling and happy. That's all I wanted. Love. Happiness.

The fact that I felt scared about telling my mother wasn't right. She should be happy that I'd finally found someone who liked me for me. Not because of what I could do for them. Or for my money or my connections. Noelle didn't give a shit about that stuff.

All she cared about was me.

And I *loved* her.

# chapter nineteen

## Noelle

With a trembling hand, I smoothed my red dress over my stomach and took a shaky breath. Riley was late picking me up, and I was trying not to let my mind go crazy on all the possibilities that could have happened between now and when I'd left Riley at the courthouse. I tried to focus on something else, like Emily.

Due to conflicting panels today, I hadn't been able to find her. I'd thought she would be happy for me, but after a whole day of unanswered calls and messages, I couldn't think that anymore. And I didn't blame her for being upset.

It had taken Roger and me six years of serious dating before he asked me to marry him, and even then I'd thought about it for three weeks before saying yes. And after that, our engagement had lasted a few more years, because I'd wanted to take our time.

Be sure.

But Riley asked me to marry him after days of knowing each other, and I'd said yes. On top of that, I'd actually *married* him already. I was married again.

I pressed a hand to my stomach. It had alternated between nervous butterflies about our wedding night, and nausea at the idea of meeting his mother. And no matter how much I tried not to think about it, I couldn't help but think that I hadn't even gotten a wedding night with Roger.

He'd married me, gone to the store, and then died.

It wasn't fair. It was sad. Horrible.

And I was terrified something bad would happen tonight. That I wouldn't get my wedding night with Riley, one way or the other. It had happened once, what would stop it from happening twice? I shook my head, trying to shut off my mind. It was being silly, paranoid, and scared. Even if Riley *was* already ten minutes late.

Riley wasn't Roger. He was a different man. I had to shake off this feeling that something awful would happen, and enjoy the day for what it was. My wedding day.

And this time, nothing would ruin it.

We had to get the *telling people* part out of the way, and then people would leave us alone to live our lives. We could find a place to live, figure out what I was going to do with my career, and I'd tell him my dirty little secrets about my past.

Someone knocked on the door, and I opened it with a big smile on my face. He was here, and he was okay, and thank God for that. But when I opened the door, instead of seeing Riley, Emily stood there, a bottle of wine in her hands.

"Oh my God, this has been the day from hell. I lost my phone, so I had to go to the store to get a new—" She looked me up and down. "Wow, you look pretty. I was going to suggest a quiet night in the room with a bottle of wine after my horrible day, but I see I'm too late for that."

"Th-Thanks." I opened the door wider, trying to quiet the unease roiling in the pit of my stomach. "Come in. I've been trying to call you all day."

Emily came inside, her eyes scanning the millions of flowers in my room. "I figured. I tried to come by a few times to let you know my phone was missing, but you weren't here. Uh...what the hell happened in here?"

"Riley." I smiled. "Riley happened."

She hadn't been ignoring me. She just hadn't gotten my messages. Maybe she wouldn't be angry with me at all. But she hadn't even known, and maybe she would have come with me. If she'd known.

"Oh my God." She set the wine down and walked over to one of the bouquets. The pink lilies. "The man doesn't do anything halfway, does he?" she asked, her voice tinged with a little bit of sarcasm. That was new. I wasn't sure what to do with it.

"No. He doesn't." I swallowed hard, my heart racing. "About that..."

"I can't believe you didn't tell me who he was."

I blinked. "What do you mean? I introduced him to you."

"Not *that*. He's Senator Stapleton's son. Best friends with Senator Wallington's daughter—the one who almost died when she got shot. You know, the possible future president and vice president?" Emily turned back to me. "Did you know all of that?"

Staggering back, I pressed a hand to my stomach. That's why he'd looked so familiar to me. All the pieces fell into place, making my head spin a thousand miles a minute. "No. He...he can't be."

"Yeah." Emily watched me closely. "He is."

I shook my head. The man I'd fallen for, the man that I'd married, was a senator's son. And not just any old senator's son, but a possible *vice president's* son. This was...this was unacceptable. Awful. He'd married the daughter of two killers, and he didn't even know it. He couldn't remain married to me. Not with his father's career on the line.

It was over. We were over.

We never should've gotten married.

Shaking my head in disbelief, I asked, "Where did you see all of this?"

"There was a news story tonight on them. He was spotted out at lunch, and there are whispers that he's getting back together with his fiancée. Did you know he cheated on her? Was it with you?" Emily sat on the bed. "Do you know anything about that?"

My heart sank. First, the news that he was a senator's son, not a lawyer's son, and now this? But it couldn't be true. And *he* hadn't cheated on *Sarah*. She'd cheated on him.

I was sure of it. That's what Riley had told me.

"No. He's not. He's...it's not possible."

Emily looked at me, her eyes sad. But under the sadness was anger. She looked as if she was ready to kill Riley on my behalf. "When I was in the phone store, I saw him on TV. It said he and his fiancée were spotted at lunch today. There were pictures of them hugging. It was tied to that story about Senator Wallington's daughter and the shooting." She lifted a shoulder, stiffening and glowering at the flowers. "I can't believe he sent you all these, then went out to lunch with his fiancée. What the fuck? Who does that?"

None of this seemed real. I sat down on the bed. Why would he have done that? He'd married *me*, not *her*. "They went out on a...date?"

"Yeah." Emily reached out and grabbed my hand. "You okay? I know you liked him a lot, but did he lie to you and tell you he was done with her? I'll kick his..." She froze, her face going pale. "Wait a second. What is that on your finger?"

I swallowed hard, knowing what she'd seen. My ring. It was pretty hard to miss. "It's a ring. A...wedding ring."

"No." Emily let go of me. "You didn't."

I lowered my head. "I did."

Emily lurched to her feet, scowling down at me. "You *married* him days after meeting him? Without even knowing who he really was? Are you kidding me?"

When she put it like that, it sounded stupid. But at the time, it had seemed right. Perfect even. "I—"

"I'll kill him." Emily headed for the door with long strides, every inch of her exuding anger. "He tricked you into marrying him, and then went out with some floozy? That son of a bitch."

"Emily, wait! I—"

She threw the door open, and Riley stood there. When he saw me, he smiled and opened his mouth, his green eyes sparkling like normal. "Hey, sorry I'm late. I got hung up with—"

Emily pushed his shoulders, and he stumbled backward. "We know where you were, damn it. And who you are, too. How *dare* you?"

He slammed into the wall, his eyes wide. "I'm sorry you're upset, but I didn't marry her to hurt you. I swear it. I really care about—"

"Shut up." Emily shoved his shoulders again. "Just shut up. How could you do this to her?"

Riley looked at me, his brow wrinkled, and held his hands up in the air. "What did I do, besides marry her?" He tore his gaze off Emily and looked at me. "What's going on, Noelle? Tell me what's wrong so I can fix it."

"Is he seriously going to play dumb?" Emily asked, more to herself than to me, I was sure. "I warned you not to hurt her. Told you she'd suffered enough pain already. Well, you didn't listen. Now you'll answer to me."

I swallowed hard. "You were all over the news today with your... your...ex-fiancée."

"What?" He blanched. "No. It wasn't like that. We went to lunch, yes, because I told her about us. It was strictly platonic, and we needed to figure out what to do with the house...it was completely innocent. I swear it. Nothing happened."

Emily laughed. "Unbelievable."

I shook my head, backing up and tugging on my necklace. I didn't know what to think, but I had a hard time believing he'd marry me, and then immediately go out on a romantic date with his ex. That wasn't the Riley I knew. His explanation made more sense. "Then why was it on TV?"

"I have no idea." He gave Emily a look out of the corner of his eye, skirted around her, and crossed into the room. "But I'd never, ever cheat on you. You have to believe me."

I swallowed hard. I wanted to so badly. "Why would they show it then? And say you two were getting back together?"

"Because it's true?" Emily snapped. "Seriously, do you believe him?"

Closing my eyes, I shook my head. "I don't know what I believe anymore."

"Noelle, don't. Don't do this. Don't think I cheated on you." He held his hands out for mine, those green eyes I loved so much locked on me. We were both avoiding the other issue—his true identity. "I didn't do anything with her. I wouldn't. Noelle…"

Staring at him, I stopped fidgeting with my dress. "Yeah?"

"If you ever doubt anything about me," he said, stepping even closer to me, and I didn't back up this time, "don't doubt my faithfulness to you. I would never do that to someone I care about, and I care about you. A lot."

I nodded, biting my lower lip. Deep down I knew he was telling me the truth. I just knew. "Okay."

"Okay?" he asked, looking a little taken aback. "Does that mean you believe me?"

I looked at Emily, who watched with wide eyes. "Yes, I do."

"Oh, thank God." He closed the distance between us, picking me up in his arms and hugging me tight. "I don't like the feeling I got in the pit of my stomach when you thought I'd done that."

I buried my face in his neck, breathing in his scent. He smelled like the beach and cologne. An intoxicating combination. "Me neither."

"You're married," Emily said quietly. "You're actually married."

Riley set me down, his hands lingering on my hips. "We are. We tried to tell you."

"My phone was lost, so I went to get a new one." She shook something off, staring back at Riley. "You didn't cheat on her?"

"I didn't." He placed a hand over his heart. "I swear it. And I never will."

Emily nodded once. "I think I believe you."

"You're not a lawyer's son." I swallowed hard. "You're…you're…"

"He was a lawyer before he was a senator. That was true. But, yes, my father is a senator, and he's running for vice president with Carrie's father. I'm sorry I didn't tell you right away, but I liked that you didn't know." He caught my hands in his. His touch felt so right, so perfect, but his words were shattering everything apart. "In my world, that's all anyone ever sees. My father. But you liked me for me, and I didn't want to lose that. I'm sorry for not telling you the truth right away."

My heart shattered. He was apologizing for not telling me about his parents, but he didn't know I hadn't told him about mine.

"Noelle..." Emily said, clearing her throat.

"I know." Taking a shaky breath, I said, "Riley, you don't know the full truth about my past, either, though. I'm—"

"I want to hear all of this. I do." Riley checked his watch. "But we're late. Can we talk later? Everyone is waiting for us at the dinner, and I don't want to make them angry before we even tell them the news."

Emily cleared her throat. "Uh, sorry I hit you, Riley. I believe you're telling the truth." She locked eyes with me. "About *everything*."

Riley didn't take his gaze off me. "It's okay. If I'd really cheated on Noelle, I'd have deserved that and more. You were only looking out for your friend."

"My sister." Emily grabbed her purse. "Which makes you my brother now. So...yeah. That's that."

Riley caught her hand as she passed. "We're going to a dinner to tell my mother and a few friends about our marriage. Mostly family. Would you like to come with us?"

"I wouldn't want to intrude."

"You wouldn't be intruding." He caught her gaze. "Like I said, it's mostly family, sister."

Emily's cheeks flushed. "Um, sure. Why not? But I'll take my own car, because I have to be back by eight."

"Great." He squeezed me one more time. He looked me up and down, his eyes burning a path everywhere they touched. "You look gorgeous, by the way. I'm the luckiest man in the world."

My stomach tightened in knots. "Thank you."

We locked gazes, still holding each other, neither one of us speaking.

"Oh my God." Emily fanned her cheeks. "I'm glad I'm driving separately from you two. You're, like, oozing sex pheromones."

"Sorry," I mumbled. My cheeks grew hot, and I forced my eyes off him. "So sorry."

Riley laughed and let go of me. "I'm not. Not really."

Emily grinned. "I don't think either of you are, and you shouldn't be."

"We know that." Riley nodded. "We just hope everyone else agrees."

"Will this dinner be rough?" Emily asked.

"Yes," I said.

"No," Riley said. Then he winced. "Okay, probably. My mother has always had very clear visions of the woman I'd marry, and..."

"I'm not her," I said, smiling at Riley. "It's okay, we both knew that."

"I know, but she's wrong." Riley cupped my cheeks. "You're her.

She might not know it yet, but I knew it the second I saw you. You're the one."

I smiled even bigger. He was just so sure. So happy, it was hard not to. "I know. The feeling is mutual."

"Geez." Emily eyed us. "You got any brothers?"

Riley laughed. "Nope. Lots of single friends, though." He paused. "One is Scottish."

Emily straightened. "Scottish, you say? The one from your office?"

"Mmhmm." Riley glanced at me with laughter in his eyes. "He'll be there tonight."

"Sold. Let's go."

Riley entwined his fingers with mine, looking down at me with a serious expression. He held me back, letting Emily leave the room without us. "Everything's going to be okay. It's just a dinner."

I nodded, but I knew it wouldn't be okay. On the way to dinner, I had to tell him the truth, and he had to decide whether or not to announce our marriage.

And I had the distinct feeling it would be the latter option.

# chapter twenty

### Riley

Next to me in the limo, I could feel the tension rolling off Noelle like a tangible thing. She'd been quiet ever since she'd found out who I really was, and my mind was going so many different places with it. Maybe she hated the fact that my father was a senator. Maybe she was from the other political party and was disgusted.

The sensible voice in the back of my mind, the one I'd been ignoring since I met her, whispered that if I'd gotten to know her before marrying her, then maybe I wouldn't be so nervous about her silence. But I flipped him off and told it to go fuck himself. I was done being sensible and doing what was expected of me.

That was the old me. The new me didn't play that way.

The other voice in my head whispered that it was probably because she'd married me on a whim, when she didn't love me, and now she regretted it. That she wished she hadn't, because she was missing her husband. Her real husband.

And that hurt like hell.

The car turned down the road that led to the restaurant. Emily followed behind us in her own car, so we were alone. I'd gotten a limo because it was our wedding night. We might not be doing things the traditional way, but on the way home from this dinner I was making love to my wife in the limo.

That much I knew.

The rest was completely wide open and unplanned. After a whole lifetime of knowing exactly what I was going to do with my life—whether or not I wanted to do it—the uncertainty was equal parts terrifying and exhilarating. So was this whole love thing.

"Noelle—"

"Riley—"

We both broke off and laughed.

"Go on," I said.

"No, you." She motioned toward me. "Please."

"I just wanted to tell you how much I...I...I care about you." *Love you. Say it, you idiot. Say the words for the first time in your pathetic life.* "I... Nothing bad is going to happen tonight. I know this must be bittersweet for you, and so fucking different from your first wedding, but you lost the man you loved more than life itself, and that sucks. I can't ever replace him in your heart, and I won't try to. But I hope that someday you can learn to maybe love me even a fraction of the amount you loved him. If doesn't even have to be love. It can just be—"

She undid her seatbelt. "Shut up."

"What?"

Climbing onto my lap, she tugged my head back by my hair and forced my face up to hers. "I said, shut up. I care about you, too, a lot. More than I thought I ever would anyone else ever again. Don't think I don't, because I do. No one else ever made me feel the way you make me feel." She locked gazes with me. "No one. *Ever.*"

She stared down at me, the truth of her words shining in her eyes. But beneath that, there was something else. It took me a second to recognize it, but once I did, I knew exactly what I was seeing. Fear.

"Babe, what's wrong?" She straddled me, and I was inches from heaven, and all I could think about was her feelings. Love was crazy as shit. "Talk to me."

She bit down on her lower lip. The car stopped. "My parents. They're not like yours at all, and I don't think you're going to like what they were. Riley, they're not dead. They're in—"

The limo door flew open, and my worst nightmare came to life. "Riley, dear, hurry up. You're—" My mother broke off, speechless for once in her life.

Finding a woman straddling me in a limo must do that.

I glanced over Noelle's shoulder, not bothering to push her off me. She dropped her forehead on my shoulder, but I refused to feel ashamed. It's not as if we were naked or anything indecent. And she was my wife.

"Late. We know. Give us a second?" I asked, my voice perfectly calm and polite the whole time.

"Who is that on top of you?" Mom hissed, her cheeks red. "How dare you bring a...a...*hussy* to dinner."

Noelle groaned, her whole body tense, and I frowned at my mother. "She's not a hussy, Mother. She's my —"

"Riley, no!" Noelle called out.

"Wife. Her name's Noelle."

My mother staggered back as if I'd struck her. "Excuse me?"

"You heard me." Reaching over, I caught Noelle's hand. I had no idea why she'd tried to stop me from saying it, but that was a conversation for another time. "We're married. That's why we're having dinner tonight."

Noelle struggled to slide off me, and I helped her. Once she was sitting upright, she pulled her dress down to her knees and smoothed her hair. She offered my mother a small smile, but she held herself so tensely that I was sure she'd shatter into pieces. "It's nice to meet you in person."

Mom didn't even look at her. She just stared at me, not even blinking. "Excuse us for a second, please."

Noelle nodded, rising as best as she could in the limo. I couldn't help but notice how relieved she looked to be excused from the conversation. "Yeah. Of course. I'll just —"

"Sit down," I commanded, my voice a lot harder than I'd ever used with her, but not intentionally. "Don't even think about walking away from me right now."

"Okay." She sat and blinked at me. "I won't."

Mom practically convulsed. "Riley Morgan Stapleton, you and I will —"

"If you want to talk to me, then talk." I tightened my grip on Noelle and slid out of the limo. Noelle followed me wordlessly, not that she had much choice. I wasn't about to let go of her. "But she's not going anywhere."

"Fine. You want to make a scene? We'll make a scene." She glanced around, checking to see if anyone was watching us. They weren't. Once she saw this, she faced us both, her fists clenched at her sides. "You told me she was nothing to you. I specifically asked you what you were doing messing around with a girl like her, and you told me, and I quote, that 'it was nothing.'"

Noelle looked at me, her eyes wide. "Wait, what?"

"It was after I read your note, when I thought we were done," I said quickly. Squeezing her hand tighter, I turned back to my mom. "That changed. Things changed."

"Obviously." Mom crossed her arms. "This won't work, though. You have to get an annulment before the media finds out about this."

"Not happening," I said, squaring my jaw.

"I should have told you before, but I didn't think it would be an issue," she said, continuing on as if I hadn't even spoken. She paced back and forth, something she never did. I must have really shaken her up. "I didn't think you'd *marry* her. Who would marry a girl like her? Not *my* son. You have to fix this right away. This is unacceptable."

Noelle tugged on my hand, her face ashen. "You should really listen to her."

"What? No."

Mom continued on. "We can probably pay her off." She looked at Noelle, her nostrils flared. "How much will it take? Five hundred thousand?"

Noelle's mouth fell open. "I— What? I don't want your money."

"Six hundred thousand it is."

"Mom, stop it." I stepped in front of Noelle, trying to shield her from this. "Stop treating my wife like she's some mercenary who married me for a quick payoff."

Mom stopped pacing in front of me, her mouth pinched tight. "Funny, because her parents are. Wait, no. They weren't mercenaries. Silly me. They're *murderers*."

Noelle made a small, broken sound behind me.

"Stop these lies," I snapped.

"They're not lies," Mom said. "Ask her. Go on. I can see the resignation on her face. She knows she's been found out."

Slowly, as if stuck in a nightmare, I turned to my wife. To the woman who had shown me how much fun life could be when you had the right woman by your side. She had tears streaming down her face, and she watched me with the same fear I'd seen echoing in her eyes earlier. "I'm so sorry," she whispered.

"No." I still held on to her hand. "Tell me it's not true."

"I tried to tell you," she whispered. "After I found out who you were, I tried to tell you who I was. What my parents had done. If I'd known who you were from the beginning, I'd never have...we'd never..."

"No." I shook my head. "You told me they were dead."

Mom laughed. "Of course she did. She was trying to get her hands on your money. She knew who you were all along, and she planned to extort money out of us. Like mother, like daughter. At least she doesn't kill for her profits."

I let go of Noelle's hand, unable to believe this was happening. Everything I'd dreamed and dared to hope for was slipping out of my grip. "Oh my God."

"No! I didn't know!" she said, her hazel eyes locked on me. She swallowed hard, her stare haunting me with its emptiness. "You know I didn't know."

Mom growled under her breath. "Oh, sure you didn't. His face has been all over the news thanks to Carrie's attack and his closeness with the family, but naturally you had *no* idea about his identity. And you certainly didn't want to supplement your struggling writer's salary."

My heart was cracking into a million pieces, and nothing was going to stop it. Nothing was going to save me. I backed away from her. Her parents were murderers. Who was she? Who was I? I didn't even know anymore. "I can't believe this is happening."

"I can't either. Why did you *marry* her?" Mom threw her arms out to the sides. "This would look excellent on your father's campaign poster. 'Child of two murderers, and a BDSM author, joins the campaign for presidency.' What have you done, Riley?"

I shook my head, unable to talk. Unable to look away from Noelle, because I'd followed my dreams, and now I was going to lose it all. Everything. "You...I..." *I love you.* Covering my face, I staggered away from them both. "Shit."

Mom grabbed my arm. "She lied to you, son, and you fell for it. All she ever wanted was your money, and now she'll get it. Let me guess. You didn't sign a prenup."

My stomach clenched so tight I thought I was going to hurl right on the street in front of the restaurant. I almost wished I would.

"We did. On a napkin," Noelle said, her voice almost mechanic sounding.

"Oh my goodness." Mom groaned and held a hand to her forehead. "A napkin. This is..." She choked on a laugh. "This is too much."

I shook my head. "Mom..."

"She's got us—hook, line, and sinker," she snapped, advancing on me. I stood my ground, which was directly in front of Noelle. "You walked right into her trap."

"No!" Noelle cried, coming to my side and holding her hands out to me. She reached for me, but I moved out of range. If she touched me, I'd be unable to think clearly. Right then, in front of me, she crumbled. I saw it in her eyes. The way she swallowed a sob. I saw it, but more importantly, I felt it. I felt her pain. "You have to believe me. This wasn't a scheme to get money from you. What we had together wasn't a lie."

I covered my face, so conflicted right now. I didn't know what to think. What to feel. I wished we'd stayed in our bubble and hidden from the world. None of this would be happening if we had. "Shit, Noelle."

"I'm sorry," she whispered. I almost didn't hear her. "So sorry."

"Yeah." I gave her my back because it hurt to look at her, knowing what I had to do next. It was time to fix this, no matter how much it hurt. "Me too. We both..."

"You have to do your duty and fix this, Riley," Mom said, her voice so low it was almost scarier than a full-out yell. "Do not let this family down."

"I never do, do I, Mother?" I asked, my voice as hollow as I felt.

"Riley, please," Noelle said, her voice cracking. She reached out for me again. And I stepped back again, because if she touched me, I'd never be able to do what came next. "*Talk to me.*"

"I can't," I said, my voice hoarse and foreign sounding even to me. I'd never been in so much pain over something that didn't involve a physical blow. Hell, not even then. "It hurts too much."

She backed up, her eyes wide. "Are you saying what I think you're saying?"

"We have to fix this." Mom paced back and forth frantically. "This has to be fixed. We can't let the press get a hold of this. Riley, what have you done? Just think of what this will do to your father. To Carrie's father. To *Carrie*."

I stiffened, but my heart fell to my feet. I didn't know much right now, but I knew one thing: It was time to figure out how to make this all go away, for the sake of my father's life work. Sure, I'd been impulsive and made rash decisions, and it had felt right.

So fucking right.

But I couldn't let that impulsiveness ruin the lives of everyone around me. I couldn't do that to them. Not even if it would kill me to walk away from the one person who had made me happy, even for a short time.

"What do we need to do to fix this?" I asked Mom. She watched me as if I was the biggest disappointment on Earth, and I felt like it. "What do you need me to do?"

Noelle gasped and covered her mouth, shaking her head.

"Who married you?" Mom tossed a triumphant look at Noelle, and then straightened. "Who was the officiate?"

"Thomas."

She sagged against the wall. "Oh, thank God. He's always been loyal to us. I can convince him to sweep this whole mess under the rug before the paparazzi gets their grubby hands on it. No one needs to know."

Everything inside me screamed out to stop this madness. To grab Noelle and run for the hills. To protect what we'd grown during the past few days. But to do so would mean betraying my father and everyone else who had supported me my whole life.

"And you." Mom glared at Noelle. "I'll ask you one more time, how much money will it take to ensure you never speak of this?"

"None." Noelle lifted her chin and stared my mother down in a way that filled me with pride. "I don't want a single cent of your money, Mrs. Stapleton."

"But you must never speak of this to anyone, ever. Understood?"

Noelle dropped her hand. "Don't speak to me as if I'm some... some...idiot. Or gold digger. I never wanted this. I never wanted any of this. And yet, I'm getting it. Losing everything that mattered. The *only* thing that mattered."

My mother stared at her, as if she couldn't figure Noelle out.

That was because she'd never met anyone like Noelle.

I closed my eyes, unable to look at her for another second. If I did I might break. I might not be strong enough to do the right thing for my family. "Noelle..."

"Don't. Don't you worry about a thing." She backed up a step, her palm pressed against her heart. It made me wonder if hers hurt as much as mine did right now. "I knew this was coming the second I found out who you really were."

"This prenup...where is it?" Mom asked.

"H-Here." Noelle reached into her purse and held it out to me with a shaking hand. I almost didn't take it, because I didn't want it. I wanted Noelle. "Take it."

"I don't want it."

"You have to take it." She glanced at Mom. "Just do it."

I did. Our fingers didn't touch. After she handed me the napkin, she tugged her ring off and handed that to me, too. I took it out of reflex.

She nodded once. "I-I'll go now. Just...just let me know what I need to do."

"But—" I almost stepped closer to her, but I forced myself to stand still. My heart shattered even more, and I had a feeling it would never be put back together again. Swallowing hard, I dug my nails into my palms to stop from reaching for her. "Yeah. Okay."

Emily came up, took one look at the three of us, and stopped. "What's going on here?"

Mom looked at her with disdain. "Who are you?"

"She's my sister-in-law," Noelle said, her voice hollow.

"Oh, lovely," Mom snapped.

The door opened behind me. I knew without looking that it would be Finn and Carrie. More people to witness my shame. I closed my eyes in embarrassment.

"Is everything okay out here?" Finn asked.

"No, everything is not okay," I said between clenched teeth. "Not at all."

Carrie smiled and walked up to Noelle, offering my wife her hand. "Hello, I'm Carrie Coram."

"H-Hi." Noelle took her hand. "I'm Noelle Brandt."

"Noelle Stapleton now, right?" She smiled at Noelle. Noelle stared blankly back at her. "I hear congratulations are in order, but—"

"She's not a Stapleton," I said, my heart breaking even more as I watched Carrie befriend Noelle. I'd wanted this so bad. Wanted this little slice of happiness in my life. "Not anymore. It's over."

And just like that, everything I'd wanted slipped away...

Right in front of my eyes.

# chapter
# twenty-one

## Noelle

I hugged my arms to my chest, tears streaming down my face. This man, the one staring at me with so much pain and regret, had been my one last attempt at a happy ending. If I couldn't get it with him, I couldn't get it with anyone. He'd made me feel so much, in so short of a time, and now he was ripping it all away from me. It was over.

*So* over.

Within a matter of minutes of meeting him, he'd somehow managed to make me forget all about my years of practice at keeping people at a distance. I'd let him in, and look how it had ended. Like this. His rejection, though completely expected, hurt more than any of the horrible things his mother said.

And even worse, when he'd first found out my parents were murderers, he'd looked at me as if I was the one who murdered those people. As if I were scum, and right now I felt like I was. Because of them.

I hadn't felt this way since Connecticut.

Carrie looked at me with wide eyes, her expression filled with shock. She was even prettier than I'd imagined. No wonder why Riley had fallen in love with her. "What's wrong? What's going on?"

"We can't be together because of her past. I might have ruined things even more than when Sarah slept with another man." Riley turned his back to me, and it hurt almost as much as his words. "My actions have jeopardized our fathers' campaign, so I'm sorry."

Mommy Dearest placed a hand on his back. "It'll be fine. Thomas will help us hide it all."

*Yeah. Hide it all. Wonderful.* Why was I still standing here, listening to them planning on how best to hide our love from the world? Why couldn't I move my feet and walk away? Why couldn't I forget all of this had ever happened?

Finn stiffened beside Riley, straightening to his full height. He eyed me, but the sadness that Riley's eyes held was absent from Finn's blue eyes. "What happened?"

"She didn't tell me her father and mother were in jail for murder." Riley covered his face. "Not until after we were married, anyway."

Finn covered his mouth and rubbed his jaw, also turning away from me. "Shit, man. All right. But she didn't kill anyone. So we can—"

"*No.*" Mrs. Stapleton shook her head. "We cannot possibly find a way around this besides a quiet dissolution of the marriage."

Carrie hesitated. "Is that what you want, Riley?"

His shoulders were stiff and hard, but I still saw them tremble. "It's the only way," he said, his voice a mirror image of his mother's. It made me sick to my stomach. "We have to fix it, and this seems the best way. Thomas will keep it all quiet. No one will know anything."

All four of them turned and looked at me with varying degrees of pity, fear, and regret. I almost backed up, but then I stiffened my spine. Yes, it was awful. And yes, I was ashamed of my past because of them. But the way Riley and his mother looked at me made me feel as if *I* were the one who did it. And that wasn't fair.

"Don't look at me like that."

Carrie looked at Finn, then me. "Like what?"

"Like I'm the one who pulled the trigger, or like I'm a creature to be pitied. I'm not. I didn't hurt anyone, I don't want your money, and you can all go to hell."

"You think she wanted your money? Wow." Emily came up to my side, showing her solidarity. "You're an idiot if you think that's true."

Riley's mother rolled her eyes. "Let's stop the 'I'm so innocent' act. No one's buying it."

Riley didn't look at me. He wouldn't look at me ever again.

It was time for an exit.

Carrie stepped forward. "Let's not be rash here. No one thought Finn would work out in this family, but look at—"

"Enough," Riley's mother said. She took out her checkbook. "It's time to get rid of this problem. Six hundred thousand, right here."

"No."

Riley watched, looking a little bit green. "*Noelle.*"

We stared at each other for another second. I wanted to throw myself into his arms and beg him to hug me and love me and keep me. But instead, I walked away.

Just walked away.

"*Wait!*" Riley called from behind me.

I walked faster.

"Crap." Emily glanced at me out of the corner of her eye. "He's going to catch up to us."

Within seconds, he caught my hand, and just the touch of his fingers on my skin hurt. "Noelle, please."

"Go away," Emily snapped.

"What do you want?" I stopped, closing my eyes, and yanked free of his touch. "What more could you possibly have to say to me?"

"So much, and yet not enough," Riley said.

Emily cleared her throat. "I'll wait in the car."

His green eyes locked on mine, and he caught my hand, refusing to let go. "What happened with your parents?"

"It doesn't matter anymore." I tried to pull free, but he didn't let me. "Let *go.*"

"What happened with your parents?" he asked again, his jaw tight.

"I don't want to talk about it. I don't like people looking at me differently because of something my parents did." I tugged on my hand again, but he still didn't let go. "Just like you did. Like you are, right now."

"Shit." He tightened his grip on my hand, looking ashamed of himself. "Noelle, I—"

"You want all the details before I go? Fine. They robbed a store. The storeowner fought back. My dad shot him, right in the chest." I yanked free, swiping the tears off my cheeks angrily. I didn't like crying. Not in public. Not ever. "As if that wasn't enough, my mother decided the wife had to die, too, or else there would be a witness. She shot her." I paused, closing my eyes. The images never left me alone. They'd been blasted on the news nonstop. "I was fourteen when it happened."

He shook his head. "Jesus, that's awful."

"Yeah. You're right. It is." I hugged myself. "Is your morbid curiosity satisfied now? Can I go?"

He reached for me. "Stay. We can figure out a way around this—"

"No." I backed away from him, holding myself even tighter. I wasn't the right wife for him. I'd known it before I'd known who he was, and now it was something I'd never be able to forget. "Absolutely not."

The pain in his eyes echoed my own, I was sure. "I can't let you leave like this. I…we…we can make this work. Right? We can do this."

Oh my God, he was going to kill me. Because I wanted to, oh so badly. But this wasn't a dream or a fantasy. It was real life, and real life didn't end like the movies.

It ended in tears and pain.

I shook my head. "There's no other way for this to end, really. We're not suitable, you and I. It was fun to forget it for a little while, to live in a world of make-believe where happy endings actually exist, but it's over. We're over."

He reached for me again, and my resolve almost cracked. "*Noelle.*"

"No! You looked at me as if I were the one who killed someone," I said, putting all the pain and frustration I felt into my voice. "I won't ever forget that. You were so quick to agree to forget we ever existed, to move on."

He covered his face with his hands. "Christ, I'm sorry, okay? I panicked. I had no idea what the hell was going on. But—"

"Yeah. I know. But I did. All that time, I knew how this would end." I backed toward the car, stopping when my hand touched the handle. Even if he wanted to keep trying, to make it through this, we couldn't. I didn't belong in his world, and we both knew it. Even if we didn't admit it, we knew it. "I was just stupid enough to hope for a surprise ending, like the type I'd write. Silly, right?"

"Please." He stumbled forward, his green eyes locked on me even in the shadows of the evening light. "*Noelle!*"

Ripping the door open, I flung myself inside it. "Go, go, go!"

Emily stepped on the gas, and we took off, leaving Riley standing in the alley. He stood there, breathing heavily, and I watched him as he disappeared from view. Watched the mirror until he was too small to see, and we turned the corner that led to our hotel.

"I can't go back there. He'll come find me."

Emily hesitated. "And if he does?"

"I'll take him back. I can't take him back."

Emily nodded. "Because of the way he looked at you?"

No. I could forgive that. It was nothing more than I deserved for having parents that could do such a thing as murder two innocent people in cold blood. I couldn't take him back because I wouldn't be blasted all over the news and ripped apart on social media for a man who had married me because he'd wanted to be fun and free for a day.

Besides, he would get over me quickly enough, since he'd never really been under me. He'd get an annulment, meet an appropriate woman, and then move on. Marry her. Have babies. Live happily ever after. The mere idea stuck in my throat like a fork.

"Take me to the airport." I looked at her. "I'll give you cash for my luggage. Can you please bring them home with you?"

"Of course. Don't even think twice about that." She stopped at the light and looked at me, her brown eyes soft with concern. "But are you sure?"

I nodded, looking away from her and wiping my wet cheeks. The time for crying was over, just like Riley and I were. It was over, and I needed to go home.

Before I forgot why I was leaving in the first place.

# chapter twenty-two

### Riley

Five nights later, I stood in a hotel lounge in a tux with a cup of whiskey in my hand. All around me, people glittered in fancy dresses and diamonds. The Edison light bulbs that hung from the ceiling were ensconced in glass bulbs, and the entire room had been done up in an elaborately rich décor. The whole thing made me sick.

I was surrounded by people I'd grown up with, but I'd never felt more out of place. Next to me, Sarah chatted with a man I'd done business with a few times, and I couldn't help but wish she'd been this supportive when I'd actually wanted to marry her. During the last few days, we'd formed a friendship that we'd never had.

Platonic, of course.

But it had been forged of mutual pain and mutual loss. Speaking of loss, I glanced down at my ring finger, where the wedding ring I'd picked out still rested. I hadn't taken it off yet. To be honest, I didn't want to. After Noelle had told me she'd never forgive me, and then ran off like she had, I'd been a fucking mess. I'd raced back to the hotel, only to sit in our empty room for hours. She hadn't come back.

It hadn't taken all that long to figure out that she wasn't going to.

Sarah entwined my arm with hers, never breaking conversation, as if she sensed I might be hurting again. The pain never stopped. Sarah cast me a concerned look, and I nodded at her once. Maybe I should marry her after all. If I couldn't have Noelle, if I couldn't have true love, then who the hell cared who I ended up with as my wife?

Not me. Not her.

Obviously.

I chugged back a big gulp of my whiskey. As I lowered the glass, I saw Carrie and Finn watching me. They both looked disappointed. Oh well. I was too. Which is why I was drinking like a college kid. I finished off the rest and toasted them with the empty glass.

The room swam a little bit, but I forced my feet to stand still. To be a strong man in the storm of shit I was stuck in. Carrie pressed her mouth together and stomped across the room. Finn, like usual, followed her. He watched her with so much love in his eyes that I wanted to punch his face just for looking so damn happy.

I loved them. I did. But I loved Noelle more.

Being apart from her had showed me just how much.

They came up to me, and I excused myself from the conversation I'd never really joined. "Finn. Carrie. What a delight to see you."

"You're drunk," Carrie said, her voice hard.

"I am." I grinned. "And for the first time in five days, I actually kind of feel okay."

Finn rolled his eyes. "If you heard yourself right now, you wouldn't think that."

"Oh?" I cocked my head. "Why's that?"

"I self-medicated with pills." Finn held on to Carrie's hand, and I knew he'd come a long way if he'd admitted it like that. It had taken a lot of time, but he and Carrie had pulled through because they were in love. "You drink. You look like a fool, too."

I'd had what they had for two point two seconds, before it had all fallen apart because I'd frozen up when I'd found out who her parents really were. If I could go back to that second, I'd have acted differently. I would have told my mother to kiss my ass, that I loved Noelle and didn't care what anyone else thought, and I'd have run away with her to Canada or something. Anywhere but here, without her.

I saluted him. "Thanks, love you too, man. On that note, I think I'll get another."

"You'll need it if you want to marry *her*." Carrie eyed Sarah, her fists clenched at her sides. "What the hell are you thinking? Really?"

I wasn't going to marry Sarah, but I didn't feel like telling them that. Call me contrary, but I wanted them to think the worst of me. I deserved it for letting Noelle walk away from me. I stuck my hand in my pocket and pulled out...something.

As soon as I saw what that something was, a knife punched through my chest. It was our prenup napkin. There, in front of my eyes, was Noelle's promise to never want anything out of me besides my heart. I'd told her she already had it.

She still did and always would.

I blinked down at the object in my hand, the pain I felt ripping through me as real and as raw as the night I'd watched her walk away...and let her.

"Riley?" Finn said, a brow cocked. "You all right?"

"I—" I swallowed past my swollen throat and crumpled the napkin. With a trembling hand, I shoved the napkin back into my pocket. If only it was so easy to shove away all the pain, too. "I'm fine. What was the question again?"

Carrie reached out and grabbed my hand, squeezing it. "I asked what you were thinking, hanging out with Sarah again."

"Oh. In that case, I'm not thinking at all, and it feels fabulous." I looked at Sarah, who was still chatting up the guy whose name I couldn't remember. The prenup napkin burned a hole in my pocket. "Not thinking is underrated."

"You're an idiot," Carrie snapped. "I get that you thought you loved Noelle, and it didn't work out. But that doesn't mean—"

"I didn't *think* I loved her. I loved her. Hell, I still love her." I glared down at my empty glass. "But it doesn't matter anymore. I ruined it."

Carrie glanced over at our parents. "Wait. You *still* love her?"

"Yeah." I yanked on my tie. It was trying to suffocate me. "But even if she loved me like I loved her, I wouldn't be able to be with her."

"Why not?" Carrie asked.

"Duh." I pointed at her nose. Or, I tried anyway. "Because of you guys."

Finn smacked my hand away from Carrie's nose. "Dude."

Carrie blinked. "Us? Why?"

"Your father. My father. You." I shrugged. "The campaign."

"Oh my God." She lunged at me, and Finn caught her from behind. That didn't stop her from swinging at me. "I'm going to *kill* you."

I leapt back, my hands up and eyes wide. "Jesus, Carrie, what the hell?"

"It's the hormones. Watch out, dude," Finn said looking entirely unconcerned for my safety.

"Hormones...?" I blinked away the fog of the drink. "Wait, does that mean...?"

"Yes, you idiot," Carrie snapped. "And we weren't going to tell anyone," she said, glowering over her shoulder at Finn, who still held on to her.

"That was before you attacked one of our best friends," Finn said calmly.

I grinned. "Wow! Congrat—"

"Shut up. Just shut up." Carrie scowled daggers at me. "How dare you hide behind the excuse of saving the campaign? You know better than that. You can't live your life for the freaking campaign. I never did, so why should you?"

Finn nodded behind her, still holding on to his wife. He didn't even look as if it was a struggle, even though Carrie squirmed more than a wet cat. "She's right."

"Oh, well, silly me. Here I thought the presidency was important to our families."

Carrie stopped struggling. "More important than love? Happiness? Marriage?"

"When you put it that way…" I mumbled, cutting myself off.

Finn sighed. "Dude. Do you love her?"

"Of course I love her." I rubbed the back of my neck. "But she won't forgive me. I fucked up big time by letting my mom plan to push her under the fucking rug."

"All men mess up," Carrie said. "It's inevitable. You're all doomed to fail right from the start. It's in your DNA."

"Wait." I rubbed my eyes. "What?"

"Just go to her. Apologize and tell her you love her. Ignore the press and your parents, like you did when you married her." Carrie reached out and squeezed my hand. "I think she only left because she knew your mother wouldn't accept her. I mean, the daughter of murderers as the vice president's daughter-in-law? That's crazy."

"She didn't do it," I argued. "It's not her fault."

"I agree." Carrie shrugged. "I never said I didn't think she was good enough for you. You're the one who decided it had to end, not us."

I staggered back. She was right. I'd been so quick to fall back into bad habits. So quick to lose Noelle, and it was my fault. All my fault. "Shit."

Finn sighed. "Stop looking as if the world is over. You love her. She probably loves you. So get on a fucking plane and find her, dumbass."

My heart raced. Could I do that? Travel across the country and hunt her down? Beg for her forgiveness and hope she loved me as much as I loved her? "But—"

"No *buts*." Finn reached into his pocket. "Here's her address."

"What?" I took the piece of paper he offered me. "How did you get this?"

"It wasn't rocket science. I looked up the articles about her parents and went from there. We already knew her name and her city." Finn shrugged. "The rest was easy."

I blinked down at the address. It seemed legit. It had a Queens zip code. This was it. I could go get my happiness and refuse to let it go this time. Refuse to give in to fear, gossip, or anything else. All I had to do was convince her to forgive me.

And then she would be mine forever.

Our buddy, Hernandez, came over to our little group. Finn had invited him to the fundraiser. He looked uncomfortable and as if he felt out of place in his tight-fitted suit, and his close-shaved head was immaculate as always. Underneath that suit, he had tattoos and piercings, but you'd never guess it tonight. "What's going on over here?"

On his left was my buddy from Scotland, Wallace. The one I'd wanted to hook up Emily with. "What did we miss, besides Stapleton here making a fool of himself with the booze?"

I rolled my eyes. "Really, Wallace? Cut the Scottish brogue crap."

"In case you failed to notice, I am Scottish, good lad." He clapped me on the back harder than necessary. "Or did you not ken that?"

"I *ken* that perfectly well." I slapped his back in return. He stumbled forward. "I also *ken* you only break it out to get the ladies in bed, and there are no ladies here."

Carrie scowled at me. "Excuse me."

"Fine. No *available* ladies."

Finn grinned and threw his arm over her shoulder. "Damn straight. This lady is spoken for, very loudly and thorough—*oof*."

Carrie elbowed her husband. "I am surrounded by testosterone. Please go get Noelle to come back, and make her stay this time."

Hernandez tugged on his suit sleeves. "I thought that was over?"

"Nope, not anymore," Finn said, nuzzling Carrie's hair. "Riley still loves her."

"Ah." Hernandez rocked back on his heels. A shade of deep emotion crossed his eyes, and he glanced at something across the room. It didn't take rocket science to know what, or more precisely, *who*, he looked at. "In that case, why the hell are you still standing here? Go get her. You don't want to waste your chance at happiness."

We all fell silent.

After a bit, Wallace cleared his throat and dropped the old-fashioned language. The brogue, of course, stayed. "I've never been in love, and I don't think I ever will be. I like being single in a world full of American women fawning over my accent. Life's too short to try to narrow it down to one lucky lass."

Finn laughed. "Famous words of a man who's about to meet his match."

"Not me, laddie." Wallace grinned and scratched his red head.

"Need a ride to the airport, man?"

"Yes, please." I set the empty glass down and looked at my parents. They spoke with Sarah, looking way too fucking happy to be doing so. "But first, I have something to do."

I walked up to my parents, my steps sure and steady despite the amount of alcohol I'd imbibed. As I approached, my mother fidgeted and avoided my eyes. She'd been acting strange around me ever since Noelle happened. But, hell, I'd been acting weird around her, too. My dad had no idea what had happened, because he hadn't even been told about my marriage.

"Mom. Dad."

"Hello, son," Dad said, clapping me on the back.

"We were just talking to Sarah about your cancelled wedding." Mom smiled, but it was her fake smile. "Is it true that you didn't cancel the venue?"

Sarah cast me an apologetic look. "We just haven't gotten to it yet."

"I didn't, but I won't be getting married there. I'm already married."

Dad sputtered.

Mom scowled.

"Yeah, I married someone else." I locked eyes with my dad. "She comes from a difficult background, but she's got a heart of gold. If I can convince her to forgive me, after my blunder the other night, I'll spend the rest of my life making that up to her. So you better get the PR team on it. I'm sure you can find a good way to spin it, because I'm going to go get my wife back."

"*Riley,*" my mom managed to say. "You—"

"No. I'm not discussing this. It's not acceptable." I gave her one last look. "In fact, I find your behavior toward my wife unacceptable, and if you want to be a part of your grandchildren's lives, I'd work on that."

Without another word, I walked away. Wallace, grinning bigger than I'd ever seen him grin, waved and then followed me out the door. "Nicely said."

"Thanks." I shrugged out of my tux jacket and tossed it over my arm. "Now let's get the hell out of here before she rediscovers her voice."

I'd never felt freer than I did right here. Right now.

All I needed was my wife back, and I'd be a happy man.

# chapter
# twenty-three

## Noelle

Sighing, I struggled to unlock my door while juggling the overloaded bag of groceries in my arms. It had been a long day out and about in the city in a failed attempt to distract myself from heartache, and it had been an even longer six days without Riley in my life. The past few days had been a mixture of pain, agony, and more pain.

I prided myself on being the type of woman who didn't need a man hanging around to make me happy, or to feel complete. But without Riley? I felt *empty*.

Emptier than I'd ever felt.

It was crazy, really, when you thought about it. I'd only spent a handful of days in his company, and yet he'd left an aching hollowness in his wake. One that I was beginning to think I'd never be able to fill again. And it sucked.

I missed him so much it hurt, and it wasn't fair.

None of this was fair.

I looked down at my naked ring finger, my heart twisting. Yeah, I knew it was for the best, and all that other placid shit that made me want to punch someone, but it didn't mean it was right. Or that it was easy.

And not calling him was harder than walking away had been.

Closing my door behind me, the first thing I noticed was the lights were on in my apartment. The second thing I noticed was that I wasn't alone. I froze, reaching for the Mace I had in my pocket. But before I reached it, I stopped.

My apartment smelled like…like…spaghetti sauce and garlic. And my table had a bottle of wine on it, and two empty glasses. Criminals didn't break into your apartment to make you dinner, did they? There was only one explanation.

"Emily?" I stepped into the living room, my heart pounding loudly in my ears. My hands felt weak, so I held on to the bag tightly. "Last time you came into my apartment without warning me, I punched you. You promised no more surprise visits."

"Well, I don't know about her promises," Riley said, walking out of the kitchen with a dishrag in his hands, "but she let me in, and then left. She'd started making this dinner, and I took over for her."

The bag in my hands hit the floor. Tomatoes and apples scattered out across the floor like cockroaches, as well as my emergency stash of chocolate. "Wh-Why?"

Riley glanced down, then looked back up at me with puppy-dog eyes. "Emily said you like homemade sauce and garlic bread. For dessert, there will be apple pie. And I brought wine. Moscato. Plus—"

"*Riley*."

We stared at each other, neither one of us talking.

"I miss you." He dropped the smile, and his hands fell at his sides. "I miss you so damn much, Noelle. I'm sorry I let you go, and even sorrier I didn't defend you."

My heart twisted, because I wanted to say it was okay. I wanted to say the hell with it all and forgive him. Be his wife again. "We can't—"

"When I smile, it feels like a frown. When I laugh, it feels like a sob. When I sleep, I have nightmares. When it's quiet, I hear your voice calling my name." He stepped closer, a tiny step. "When I breathe, it hurts without you. I can't sleep. Can't think. Can't fucking live without you."

I pressed a hand to my chest, cursing at my traitorous heart to stop racing at every word he said, and took a tiny step back. "There you go, saying all the right things again. Where was that guy on our wedding night?"

"I don't know," he said, hanging his head low. "I was scared, and I was finding out all these crazy things, and I…I don't know. I just clammed up and resorted to old habits. I'm so fucking sorry."

I swallowed hard. "I know."

"Do you think you could ever forgive me?" He lifted his head and stepped closer. A big step this time. I backed up again, but I was running out of space. One more step, and I'd hit the door. "Can you let me try again? Can we do this right?"

Yes. No. God, I didn't know anymore. I tried my best to remember all the reasons we wouldn't work, but he was here, in my apartment, and all those reasons had faded away the second he spoke to me. "It's... not that easy."

He stepped closer, his cheeks still flushed. I stood my ground. "I want you back, Noelle. Screw the world. Screw them all. All that matters is you and me."

My heart picked up speed again. "Why?"

"Because you're gorgeous, inside and out. Because without you, I'm not whole. Because alone, I'll never be happy. Because you've locked your claws into me, and I can't break free. Even crazier? I don't want to. Because the second I let you walk away from me, I've been dying more and more."

"Pretty words, but not enough." I lifted my chin. "I need more."

"I wasn't finished." He stepped toward me, his green eyes flashing with determination and something else. "Because I don't want to live in a world where you're not there talking to me. Hugging me. Kissing me. I might have only known you for a few days, but they were the best fucking days of my life. I know, without a doubt, that you can make the rest of my life even better. Every second I spend with you will be a second I'll want to relive. The moment I saw you, I knew it. I knew you were the one, and I talked to you because I knew if I didn't, I'd regret it the rest of my life."

I gripped my necklace even tighter and backed up. I hit the door. There was nowhere else to go. "You were drunk outta your mind that night."

"I might have been drunk, but I knew what I saw. I saw my life standing in front of my eyes. My wife. My partner. My lover." He stepped closer, cocking a brow at me. "I only had to say hello to you, and I knew everything else would follow. I had to stay outside the store instead of going inside."

"Store?" I asked breathlessly. "We were in a hotel."

"It's a metaphor. It means—" He shook his head. "Never mind what it means. All you need to know is that I knew you weren't checking out. I was drunk, not blind." He stepped closer to me. I pressed against the door. "You have nowhere else to go."

"I could open the door. Leave again."

"Please don't. I never want to see you walk away from me again. Not like that." He closed the distance between us with one last step, but he didn't touch me. "Because I know what love is now, and I don't want to lose it. I love you, Noelle Brandt Stapleton. I love you more than I would have ever hoped possible, and I never want to lose you."

I drew in a ragged breath. "You do?"

"I do. I knew it before I kissed my bride, and I think I knew it all along. It only took a few seconds for my heart to know you were the one I wanted," he said, smiling at me tenderly. "It just took the rest of me a little longer to get the message."

My lips twitched. "Not that much longer. I mean, you *did* propose to me when your cock was in my mouth."

"I'm never going to live that down, am I?"

"Nope." Grinning, I shook my head. "I don't think so."

"That's fine. You can tease me about it every second of every day for as long as we both live, as long as you say you'll love me someday." He reached out and swept his trembling fingers over my cheekbone. With his other hand, he pulled my ring out of his pocket. "Can you ever love me like I love you?"

I nodded. "Of course I love you, you idiot. But that's not the issue. Your parents—"

"Shh." He pressed his fingers to my mouth, and they burned my lips. "Say it again."

"I love you, you idiot," I said, smiling as his eyes lit up. "I love you very, very much."

His fingers shook as he took them off my lips. "I will never get sick of hearing that. Ever."

"Riley..."

"I know my parents are an issue, but I told them I came here, and I let them know why I came. There is no doubt that you are my wife and will stay that way. The campaign will find a way to spin it, or not. I don't give a damn." He touched my cheek, his eyes filled with wonder. "Not when you love me, too."

Tears filled my eyes, and I blinked them away. "Riley..."

"I don't care what they say. We can hide in a bungalow in Europe for the rest of our lives if you want. Or we can live here. Or Montana. I don't care." He dropped down to his knees and hugged me, resting his face on my stomach. "Be mine, baby. Forgive me. Take me. Love me. *Please*."

"Yes," I whispered, threading my hands in his hair. "Yes, yes, yes."

He glanced up at me, his green eyes shining with what looked suspiciously like tears. "Really?"

"Yes." I choked on a laugh. "Really."

"Thank God." He struggled to his feet, slid my ring back on my finger, and then backed me up against the door. "I swear to never give you a reason to take that off again."

I cupped his cheeks, looking deep into his eyes, and smiled. "I swear the same."

"I never took it off. I couldn't." He grabbed my hips and hauled me up against him, as if he didn't want to let go. And I didn't want him to. "I would have worn it till the day I died. I love you, Noelle."

My heart swelled so much I was surprised it didn't burst. "I love you too."

"So much." He buried his face in my neck and inhaled deeply. "So, so much."

I dug my fingers into his bare shoulders. "The no-shirt thing was a nice touch, by the way."

"Thanks." He grinned. "My buddy Wallace thought of that."

"Riley…"

He nuzzled his nose to mine. "Yes?"

"I love you and all, and this is nice," I whispered. "But are you going to kiss me or not?"

Grinning, he tipped my head back and met my eyes. "I thought you'd never ask."

Without another word, his lips closed over mine, and he was lifting me up in the air. As he walked, I wrapped my legs around his waist, groaning with pleasure. He walked toward the bedroom but stopped only a step short. With a grunt, he pressed me against the wall and cupped my butt, squeezing me through my jeans.

His tongue stroked mine as he arched his hips into me, teasing me with his huge dick. He pressed against my core, driving my need for him higher than ever before. Now that I knew he loved me, wanted me, *needed* me, it was even more intense.

"Oh my God, yes," I moaned, burying my hands in his thick blond hair. "More, Riley. I need you now."

"Then you'll get me," he said, his voice husky with desire. "Do you have any idea how many times I've pictured this reunion? You, against a wall, begging for me?"

"*Yes.*"

His hands closed over my breasts, squeezing me with the perfect amount of pressure. "I love the way you fit inside my hand perfectly, because it proves that you were made for me. You're the one I've been waiting for my whole life."

Fumbling with his fly, I tried to undo his belt, but I was in the way. I was cock blocking myself. "So take me."

"I will." He nibbled on the side of my neck, and I whimpered. He rolled his hips against me again, and the whimper turned into a strangled groan. "But this is our first make-up sex of our marriage. I'll be damned if you're going to rush me through it."

Without warning, he dropped his hold on me and my feet hit the ground. I'd barely touched the wood before he spun me around, face-first against the wall outside my bedroom. I plastered my hands on it, and he cupped my hips.

"*Riley.*"

From behind, he pressed his cock against my butt, hard and rough. "You want it fast and rough, don't you, babe? You want my cock buried inside of you now."

I nodded, biting down on my lip. "Yes. God, *yes.*"

"Well, you're going to have to wait for it." Gripping the hem of my shirt, he tugged it up. I lifted my hands over my head, letting him take it off. As soon as it was over my head, his fingers were on the clasp of my bra. It hit the floor, and then he was behind me again, covering my body with his and pressing me against the wall. I gasped when the cold plaster hit my bare nipples. "Hands against the wall. *Now.*"

I did as I was told, gasping when he bit down on the back of my neck. His fingers trailed over my bare stomach and to the button on my jeans. "You look so hot, standing there. Waiting for me to fuck you." He wrapped his belt around one wrist and then the other, securing my hands over my head. "I think I promised to use this on you, and I never did."

"That's right...you did," I said, closing my eyes. "In the hotel."

He laughed huskily in my ear. "You want me to fuck you tonight, not make love to you. I can see it in the way you're fidgeting, trying to press your thighs together. It won't work. Nothing but my cock inside your pussy will ease that ache, babe."

"Riley, God," I whispered. "I need you to take me."

"Oh, I will." He undid the button on my jeans, and then the zipper. "And when I'm done, I'll do it again, only slowly. I'll make love to you all night long. How's that for a promise?"

I nodded again, loving his words but hating them at the same time. He was killing me with the suspense. "Y-Yes."

He peeled my pants off my body, inch by inch. When they were off, he cupped my core from behind, his fingers dipping inside me. "You're not wearing any underwear, Mrs. Stapleton."

"I know." I dropped my forehead on the wall. "I left them off because of you. I know how much you liked it when I didn't wear any, so it reminded me of you."

"Did you touch yourself?" He slid a long finger deeper. "Like this, and pretend it was me?"

I nodded, squeezing my eyes shut with embarrassment.

"Say it. Tell me."

"I thought of you and...touched myself." My cheeks heated, but that was nothing compared to the heat he was causing me. "But it wasn't enough. Not even close."

He rubbed his thumb against my clit and moved his fingers. "I'll make it better. I'll take away that ache you feel. I know you do, because I feel it, too."

"I do." I rolled my hips against his fingers, stars already starting to form behind my eyelids. "I need you so bad."

"Hm." He inserted another finger, his thumb pressing against my aching clitoris as he did so. His chest pressed against my back, his hard muscles boxing me in against the wall. "Your pussy is so wet for me. So fucking hot. So fucking *mine*."

A gasp escaped my lips, and I knew I was close. So close. "Yes. Oh my God, yes." He pulled away from me without warning—taking his fingers and his mouth and his touch with him. I lowered my bound arms and tried to turn around to face him, but he didn't let me. "*No*."

"Yes. Hands up on the wall, I said." I followed instructions, gasping when the leather of his belt bit into my skin, and he clucked his tongue and undid his zipper. My insides quivered at the sound. "Good girl."

"Riley…"

"I know, babe. I know." He came up behind me, and his dick brushed my bare ass. He slipped it between my thighs, rubbing up against my core. "I'm right here, baby."

A whimper escaped me. "Please, Riley. *Please*."

He fisted my hair and placed a hand on my hip. "Hold on tight."

"Oh my God." My nails scraped the painted wall, but there was nothing to hold on to. "*Yes*."

Positioning himself behind me, he slid into me inch by slow inch. "Shit, I can't wait anymore. I need you. I love you. I need you so fucking bad."

I nodded, but he didn't take me. He caressed his hands over my body, squeezing my nipples and then lowering down over my clit. The second he touched me I tensed. "Yes. Oh my God, yes."

Stars burst in front of me, and I came, from one thrust. That's how badly I'd needed him. How badly my body had needed him. He cursed under his breath and closed his hands over my breasts. "Hands on the wall."

I flattened my hands on the plaster. "Riley, *now*."

He moved inside me. Fast. Hard. Just like he'd promised.

This time, he held nothing back from me. He knew I could handle all of him, and he gave it to me. As he made love to me, his fingers moving over my breasts and his low voice saying dirty things in my ear, the pressure built higher and higher until I was sure I'd burst. But the whole time, he was there with me.

Loving me.

His hard, sleek body was coated with a thin sheen of sweat, and he tipped my hips up so I'd take even more of him in. I hadn't even thought that was possible. He drove inside me hard. Once. Twice. On the third time, I screamed, my whole body convulsing around his hard shaft.

"Noelle," he said, his voice an uttered groan.

He pushed one last time, his grip on me tight, and then he stiffened, his whole body going tense. After a few seconds, he grunted and collapsed on me, pressing me deeper into the wall. His arms cradled me so I didn't get squished, but I didn't care. I felt way too good to care.

His ragged breathing matched mine, and he dropped a kiss on my shoulder. "You can put that in one of your books, if you'd like."

I choked on a laugh, and then he joined me, his hot skin rubbing up against mine as we both giggled like school kids, naked in my hallway. "I just might. Your mother would love that."

"Please, my mother probably read your books." He gently undid my hands, dropping the belt on the floor. "She loves romance books."

I banged my forehead on the wall. "No."

"Yes." He kissed my shoulder and lifted me in his arms, carrying me into the bedroom. "What's your pen name again?"

"K.M. Reed."

"No shit." He laughed and looked down at me in wonder. "Carrie reads your books. Finn told me she likes it when he reads her a scene out of it, and then they—"

"Oh my God, stop." I covered his mouth. "Don't say it. I'll never be able to look at them again."

He tossed me on the bed, grinning when I bounced. "Why not? That's kind of sexy."

"Oh my God." I closed my eyes. He took advantage of my distraction and leapt on top of me, covering my body with his. The second he was on me, he thrust inside me, groaning when he was fully ensconced. "Riley."

"I'm here, babe." He kissed me gently, smoothing my hair off my face. "The sauce is simmering, and the pie is cooling. The only thing you need to worry about is how I'll get you off next." He lowered his body over mine, kissing a path as he went. "And I know just where to start..."

Threading my fingers through his hair, I closed my eyes and smiled bigger than ever before. "Have I told you how much I love you lately?"

"I love you too. More than the air, and the stars, and the sky. More than life. More than anything, anywhere, ever." He nipped my hip. "Thank you for loving me."

Tears filled my eyes. "You're welcome."

And after that, words weren't possible. I was too busy counting all the lucky stars that swam before my eyes, one gentle kiss at a time...

# epilogue

## Riley

*One year later*

My fingers flew over the keyboard so fast I wasn't even sure if I was typing real words. It didn't matter. All that mattered was getting the last word on this page before Noelle did. All that mattered was winning, damn it. The waves of the Pacific Ocean crashed behind us, but I tried to tune them out. It was a beautiful southern California evening, but we were engaged in battle, damn it.

And I wanted to win.

She laughed and typed beside me, her feet entwined with mine. "I'm so going to beat you, rookie."

"Never," I mumbled, not taking my eyes off the screen. "The stakes are too high."

She got quiet, her fingers typing as furiously as mine, and I stole a glance at her. Her long blonde hair was pulled back in a ponytail, and she had a pair of grey sweatpants on, paired with a baggy T-shirt of mine. She didn't have any makeup on…

And she was sexy as hell.

We'd been married for more a year now, and we were blissfully happy. My parents had been slow to come around, but once the public heard that I'd married a "normal" woman, just like Carrie had married a "normal" man, the polls had taken a turn for the better. And so had my parents' acceptance.

Stupid, but whatever.

We were together, we loved each other, and we were happy. That's all that mattered in the end. Just us.

"You're looking at me instead of your book," she said, her plump, red mouth curving up into a smile. "Which is why I'm going to win."

"I can't help it," I said. "I like looking at beautiful things."

Her grin widened. "Said the man who didn't win."

"Oh, I won." I closed my laptop and shoved it aside. "I have you, don't I?"

Her fingers froze on the keyboard. "You have to finish your book. You're so close."

"I did. It's done." I closed her laptop, and she hurried to remove her fingers from the keys. "I won."

"Prove it," she said, her eyes narrow.

I cocked a brow at her. "Are you saying you don't believe me, your own husband?"

"Yes. I am. What were the last words you wrote?"

"The end."

"No one writes that at the end of books," she scoffed.

"I did." Grabbing her legs, I yanked her down to the floor. She cried out, but I caught her in my arms. "I win, which means I get to be in control all night long."

"First of all, that wasn't the deal we made. Second of all, you finished your book," she said, her hazel eyes shining. "You did it. I'm so proud of you, Riley."

"We can talk about that later," I whispered, lying on top of her. "I believe I was promised a reward if I finished first."

She snaked her arms around my neck. "I did promise that."

"It's time to deliver, Mrs. Stapleton." I nibbled on her ear, slipping my hand under her ass and hauling her closer to where I wanted her. "What's my reward?"

"It'll take a long time to deliver it," she said, arching her neck for me. I bit down on it, and she gasped. "Like, a really long time."

"Even better," I said, tugging her pants down. She lifted her hips, and I yanked them off her. She wasn't wearing any underwear. I loved it when she did that. "Tell me more."

"It's...it's... Oh my God." She threaded her hands in my hair. "Riley, *yes*."

I slid down her body, slipping out of my pants as I did so. The second they were off, I flicked my tongue over her clit, groaning at her sweet taste. I'd never get over this. Over her. "You want it so fucking bad, but you're not getting it yet." I trailed my finger over her slit, and then thrust it deep within her pussy. She cried out. "Keep talking, baby. What's my reward?"

"It'll take a long time to deliver your reward," she gasped, writhing beneath me. "Like, nine months, to be exact."

"Mmhmm." I moved my fingers and bit down on her neck. "I wasn't planning on taking that long, but if you insist…"

"*Riley*." She smacked my arm. "Nine. Months."

"Yeah, and—" My fingers froze. "Wait. Are you telling me you're pregnant when my fingers are inside of your pussy?"

She choked on a laugh, covering her mouth. "Oh my God, yes. I am."

"Holy fucking shit." I dropped my forehead on her stomach, taking a deep breath. "Seriously? It's true?"

She locked eyes with me, her laughter dying down. "Yes. It's true. We're having a baby."

"Holy shit," I repeated, a huge grin breaking out over my face. "Seriously?"

She nodded again, her hazel eyes shining with love, happiness, and excitement. "Yep. I wouldn't joke about this."

"Oh my God," I whispered, resting a hand on her flat stomach. "A baby. A real fucking baby."

"Well, maybe we shouldn't call it that," she teased, her dimples popping out. "But yes. A baby."

"Thank you." I crawled up her body and cupped her face, locking gazes with her. "Thank you so much for loving me. For being you. For having me, and our baby."

"No, thank you," she whispered. "For asking me if I was checking out."

"I knew you weren't." I kissed her, brushing my lips across hers. Happiness, so much fucking happiness, filled me until I was sure I'd burst. "I just had to know you."

"I know," she whispered, opening her legs. I slipped between them, nestling myself at her core. "Oh, believe me, I know. Now love me."

Kissing her again, I slipped inside of her and made love to her.

My wife. My life. My love. The mother of my child.

Life didn't get any better than this.

It just didn't.

# THE END

# about the author

Jen McLaughlin is the New Times and USA Today bestselling author of sexy New Adult books. Under her pen name Diane Alberts, she is a multi-published, bestselling author of Contemporary Romance with Entangled Publishing. Her first release as Jen McLaughlin, Out of Line, released September 6, 2013, hit the New York Times, USA Today and Wall Street Journal list. She was mentioned in Forbes alongside E. L. James as one of the breakout independent authors to dominate the bestselling lists. She is represented by Louise Fury at The Bent Agency.

Though she lives in the mountains, she really wishes she was surrounded by a hot, sunny beach with crystal-clear water. She lives in Northeast Pennsylvania with her four kids, a husband, a schnauzer mutt, and a cat. Her goal is to write so many well-crafted romance books that even a non-romance reader will know her name.